- R.A. MONTGOME

CHOOSE YOUR O

FORECAST FROM
STONEHENGE

WRITTEN BY
Stephanie Phillips

BASED ON THE ORIGINAL BY
R. A. Montgomery

ILLUSTRATED BY
Dani Bolinho

COLORS BY
PH Gomes

LETTERS BY
Joamette Gil

COVER BY
Dani Bolinho & PH Gomes

CHOOSECO

ONI PRESS

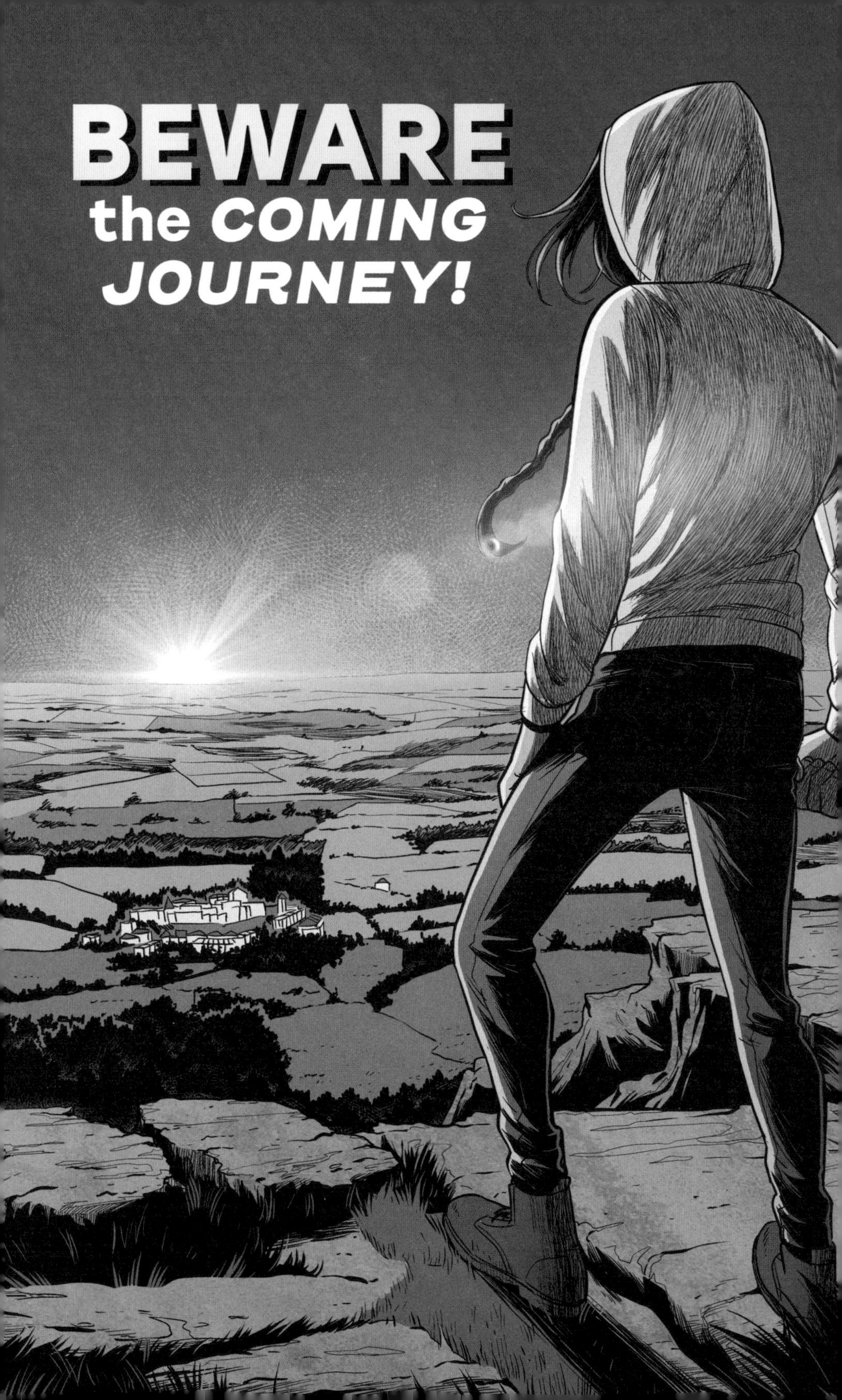
BEWARE
the COMING
JOURNEY!

This book will be different from others you've encountered,

for here, **YOU** and **YOU** alone are in charge of every decision and every pathway **YOU** take. How the story ends rests solely on **YOUR** shoulders.

The coming adventure will take **YOU** through the mystical and magical mysteries that surround the famous Stonehenge on the day of the solstice. There **YOU** shall meet a strange character named Alistair, who knows hidden secrets about the mysterious Stonehenge. Yet, because of the solstice celebration, Stonehenge is crowded with believers and tourists alike, and **YOU** must be wary and careful of each and everyone. Wizards, fairies, magic artifacts, and more all await you after each turn of the page. Within this grand tale exists many paths that can lead to riches...or mayhem.

But never fear! At any time, **YOU** may go back and make another choice. This is **YOUR** journey and no one else's. Are **YOU** ready to discover the dark secrets of the mythical Stonehenge?

DESIGNED BY Carey Soucy
EDITED BY Desiree Rodriguez & Grace Scheipeter

SPECIAL THANKS TO Shannon Gilligan & Rachel Hullett

PUBLISHED BY ONI-LION FORGE PUBLISHING GROUP, LLC.

Hunter Gorinson, president & publisher
Sierra Hahn, editor in chief
Troy Look, vp of publishing services
Spencer Simpson, vp of sales
Angie Knowles, director of design & production
Katie Sainz, director of marketing
Jeremy Colfer, director of development
Chris Cerasi, managing editor
Bess Pallares, senior editor
Grace Scheipeter, senior editor
Karl Bollers, editor
Megan Brown, editor
Gabriel Granillo, editor

Jung Hu Lee, assistant editor
Michael Torma, senior sales manager
Andy McElliott, operations manager
Sarah Rockwell, senior graphic designer
Carey Soucy, senior graphic designer
Winston Gambro, graphic designer
Matt Harding, digital prepress technician
Sara Harding, executive coordinator
Kaia Rokke, marketing & communications coordinator

Joe Nozemack, publisher emeritus

onipress.com
- facebook.com/onipress
- twitter.com/onipress
- instagram.com/onipress

CYOA.COM
- twitter.com/ChooseAdventure
- instagram.com/ChooseYourOwnAdventure
- facebook.com/ChooseYourOwnAdventure

First Edition: April 2024
ISBN 978-1-63715-245-4
eISBN 978-1-63715-848-7

1 2 3 4 5 6 7 8 9 10

Library of Congress Control Number 2022947227

Printed in China.

YOU'VE BARELY BEEN BACK HOME IN LONDON FOR TWO HOURS WHEN TWIG CALLS TO ASK FOR A FAVOR.

TWIG HAS BEEN YOUR BEST FRIEND FOR YEARS, SO IT TAKES VERY LITTLE PROMPTING FOR YOU TO DECIDE TO HOP IN A TAXI AND FOLLOW HIS INSTRUCTIONS--

STONEHENGE.

--TO MEET A MYSTERIOUS MAN NAMED ALISTAIR SHEPHERD AT STONEHENGE DURING THE SUMMER SOLSTICE TO GET INFORMATION ABOUT THE MISSING HEEL STONE.

Turn to the next page.

DESPITE FATIGUE SETTING IN JUST BEHIND YOUR EYES, THE POSSIBILITY OF LEARNING ABOUT THE MISSING HEEL STONE DRAWS YOU IN.

THE MISSING HEEL STONE IS A STONEHENGE LEGEND DATING BACK TO 1853.

THE FIRST KNOWN PHOTOGRAPH OF THE MONUMENT WAS TAKEN IN 1853, WHEN MANY OF THE STONES HAD FALLEN OVER.

SORRY ABOUT THAT!

THEN, WHEN THE HENGE WAS REBUILT IN THE 1920S, ONE OF THE STONES FROM THE 1853 PHOTOGRAPH DISAPPEARED...

...THE HEEL STONE.

Go on to the next page.

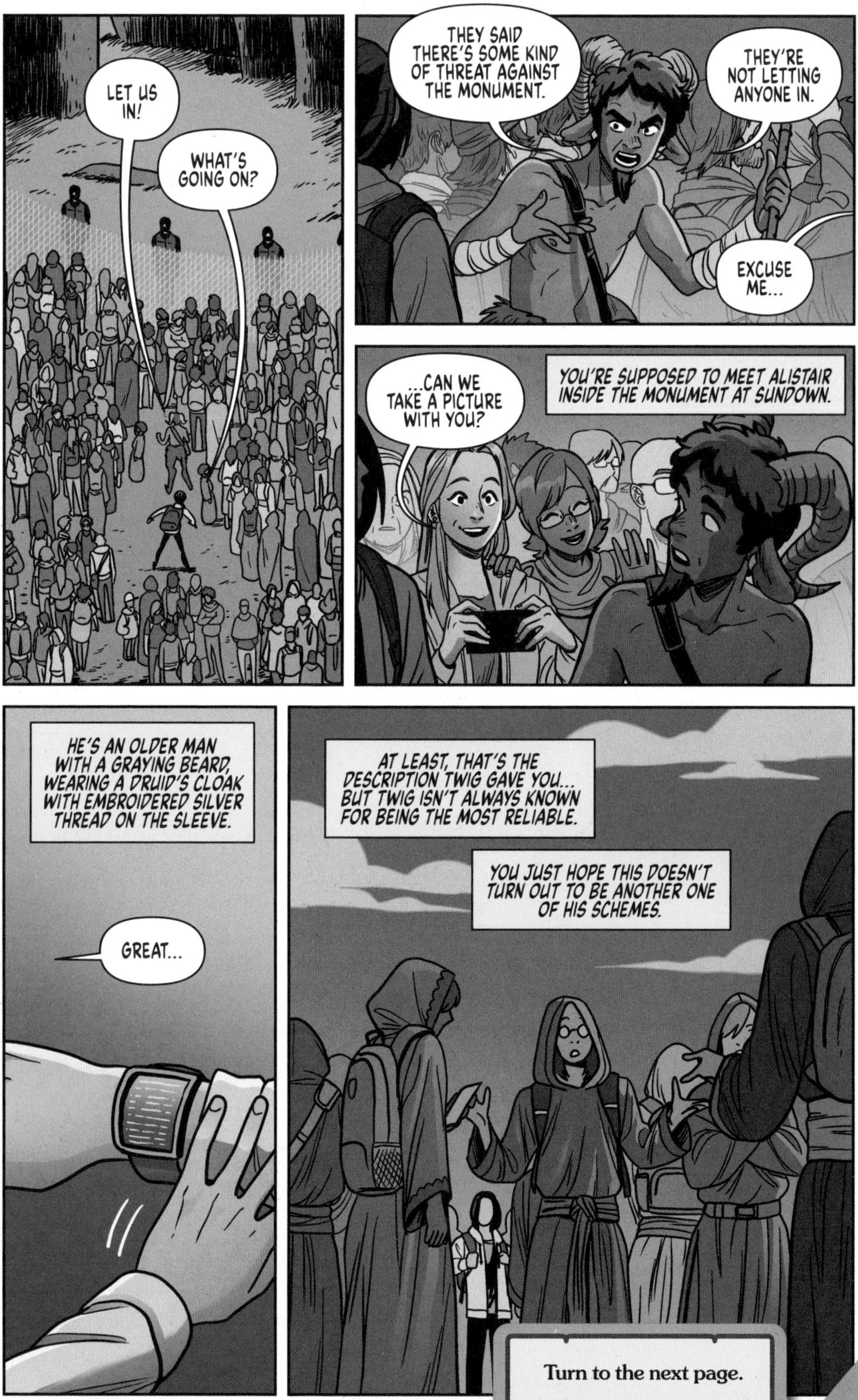
LET US IN!
WHAT'S GOING ON?
THEY SAID THERE'S SOME KIND OF THREAT AGAINST THE MONUMENT.
THEY'RE NOT LETTING ANYONE IN.
EXCUSE ME...
...CAN WE TAKE A PICTURE WITH YOU?
YOU'RE SUPPOSED TO MEET ALISTAIR INSIDE THE MONUMENT AT SUNDOWN.
HE'S AN OLDER MAN WITH A GRAYING BEARD, WEARING A DRUID'S CLOAK WITH EMBROIDERED SILVER THREAD ON THE SLEEVE.
GREAT...
AT LEAST, THAT'S THE DESCRIPTION TWIG GAVE YOU... BUT TWIG ISN'T ALWAYS KNOWN FOR BEING THE MOST RELIABLE.
YOU JUST HOPE THIS DOESN'T TURN OUT TO BE ANOTHER ONE OF HIS SCHEMES.

Turn to the next page.

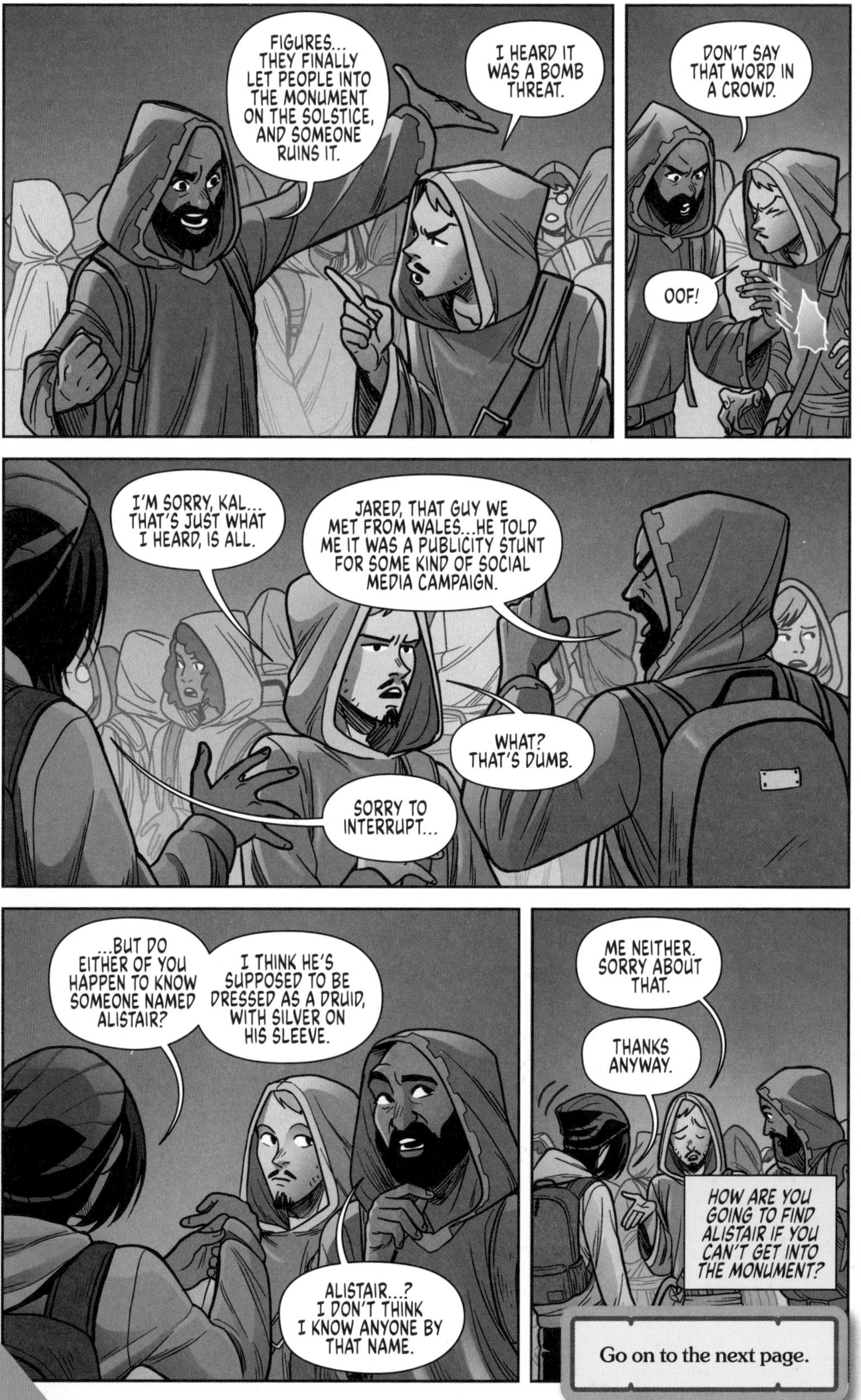
FIGURES... THEY FINALLY LET PEOPLE INTO THE MONUMENT ON THE SOLSTICE, AND SOMEONE RUINS IT.
I HEARD IT WAS A BOMB THREAT.
DON'T SAY THAT WORD IN A CROWD.
OOF!
I'M SORRY, KAL... THAT'S JUST WHAT I HEARD, IS ALL.
JARED, THAT GUY WE MET FROM WALES...HE TOLD ME IT WAS A PUBLICITY STUNT FOR SOME KIND OF SOCIAL MEDIA CAMPAIGN.
WHAT? THAT'S DUMB.
SORRY TO INTERRUPT...
...BUT DO EITHER OF YOU HAPPEN TO KNOW SOMEONE NAMED ALISTAIR?
I THINK HE'S SUPPOSED TO BE DRESSED AS A DRUID, WITH SILVER ON HIS SLEEVE.
ALISTAIR...? I DON'T THINK I KNOW ANYONE BY THAT NAME.
ME NEITHER. SORRY ABOUT THAT.
THANKS ANYWAY.
HOW ARE YOU GOING TO FIND ALISTAIR IF YOU CAN'T GET INTO THE MONUMENT?

Go on to the next page.

If you choose to stay and keep looking for Alistair outside the gates, turn to the next page.

If you decide to take Elaine's offer and go into the tunnel, turn to page 86.

THANKS, ELAINE, BUT I'LL WAIT HERE FOR ALISTAIR JUST IN CASE.

YOUR LOSS!

YOU CAN'T HELP BUT THINK THERE WAS SOMETHING A LITTLE ODD ABOUT ELAINE AND HER FRIENDS...

MOST WOULDN'T PASS UP SUCH AN OPPORTUNITY, YOU KNOW.

...BUT IT SEEMS LIKE THERE'S A BETTER CHANCE OF FINDING ALISTAIR OUTSIDE THE GATES.

THE POLICE STILL AREN'T LETTING ANYONE INTO THE MONUMENT.

AND YOU DON'T SEE ANYONE BETWEEN THE RINGS--

THERE ISN'T MUCH TIME...

Go on to the next page.

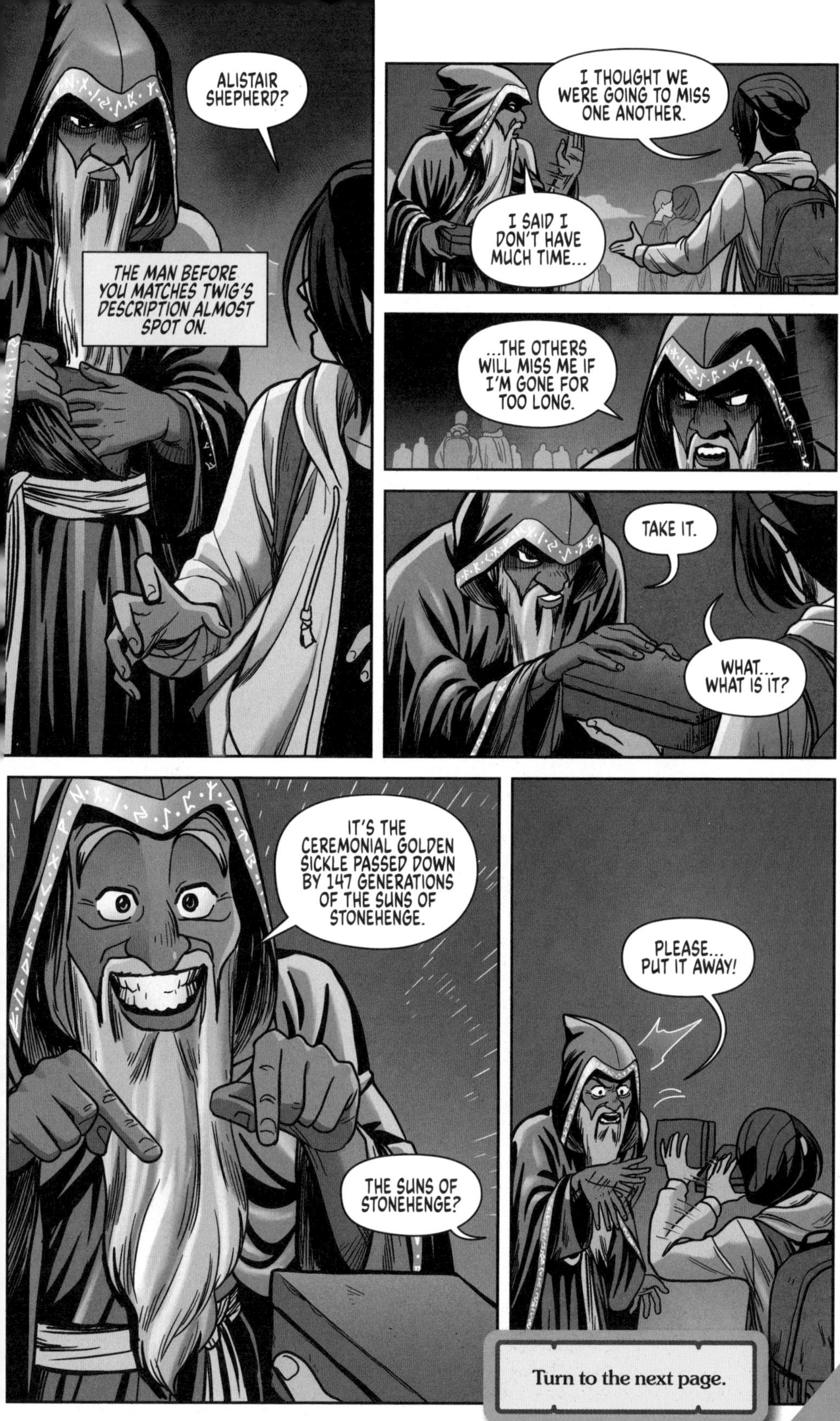
ALISTAIR SHEPHERD?
THE MAN BEFORE YOU MATCHES TWIG'S DESCRIPTION ALMOST SPOT ON.
I THOUGHT WE WERE GOING TO MISS ONE ANOTHER.
I SAID I DON'T HAVE MUCH TIME...
...THE OTHERS WILL MISS ME IF I'M GONE FOR TOO LONG.
TAKE IT.
WHAT... WHAT IS IT?
IT'S THE CEREMONIAL GOLDEN SICKLE PASSED DOWN BY 147 GENERATIONS OF THE SUNS OF STONEHENGE.
THE SUNS OF STONEHENGE?
PLEASE... PUT IT AWAY!

Turn to the next page.

I THOUGHT YOU HAD INFORMATION FOR TWIG ABOUT THE HEEL STONE.

FORGET ABOUT THE HEEL STONE.

I NEED YOU TO TAKE THE GOLDEN SICKLE TO THE BRITISH MUSEUM.

YOU MUST SEE STANDISH BLOOM, THE HEAD OF THE CEREMONIAL ANTIQUITIES DEPARTMENT.

DR. BLOOM WILL UNDERSTAND THE IMPORTANCE OF THE SICKLE.

YOU CAN DO THIS?

DR. BLOOM WILL MEET WITH ME?

YOU NOTICE THAT ALISTAIR SMELLS LIKE EARTH...LIKE DIRT OR MUD.

SEEING IT UP CLOSE, THE SILVER ON ALISTAIR'S ROBE ALMOST LOOKS LIKE IT COULD BE WRITING...

...BUT BEFORE YOU CAN TRY TO MAKE OUT THE DETAILS, ALISTAIR IS ALREADY DISAPPEARING INTO THE CROWD AROUND YOU.

JUST TELL HIM YOU KNOW ME... TELL HIM YOU HAVE THE SICKLE.

I'M BETRAYING THE GREAT OAK BY TALKING TO YOU. I MUST GO...

THE CROWD ONLY SEEMS TO HAVE GROWN SINCE THE SUN SET, AND, EXHAUSTED FROM THE LONG DAY...

Go on to the next page.

...YOU DECIDE IT'S BEST TO GET SOME REST AND PROCESS YOUR BIZARRE ENCOUNTER WITH ALISTAIR SHEPHERD.

THE NEW INN

CATCHING A RIDE INTO AMESBURY WITH A GROUP OF VERY VOCAL ELVES, YOU MANAGED TO GET THE LAST AVAILABLE ROOM AT AN INN ABOVE A CROWDED PUB.

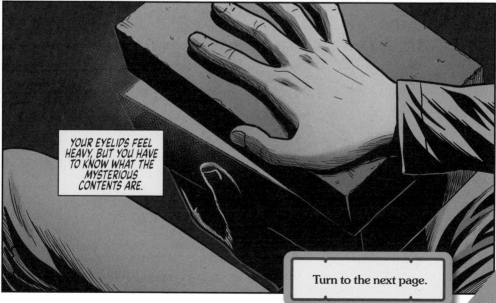

YOUR EYELIDS FEEL HEAVY, BUT YOU HAVE TO KNOW WHAT THE MYSTERIOUS CONTENTS ARE.

Turn to the next page.

SUDDENLY, YOU FORGET YOUR EXHAUSTION AS ADRENALINE KICKS IN.

YOU FEEL THE WEIGHT OF THE GORGEOUS ITEM IN YOUR HAND...ADMIRING THE SCROLLWORK ON THE SIDES AND THE BLADE'S SHARP EDGE.

MOST AMAZING OF ALL, IT TRULY IS SOLID GOLD.

OF COURSE, YOU WANT TO SEND A PICTURE TO TWIG TO SHARE THIS AMAZING ARTIFACT...

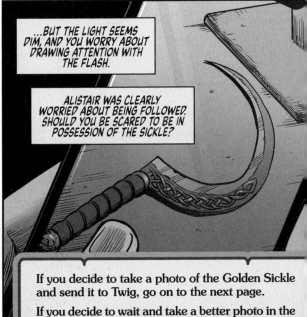

...BUT THE LIGHT SEEMS DIM, AND YOU WORRY ABOUT DRAWING ATTENTION WITH THE FLASH.

ALISTAIR WAS CLEARLY WORRIED ABOUT BEING FOLLOWED. SHOULD YOU BE SCARED TO BE IN POSSESSION OF THE SICKLE?

If you decide to take a photo of the Golden Sickle and send it to Twig, go on to the next page.

If you decide to wait and take a better photo in the morning, turn to page 18.

YOU DECIDE TO TAKE THE PHOTO NOW SO THAT IT'S WAITING IN TWIG'S INBOX WHEN HE WAKES UP.

Interesting developments... check out this photo. It's more amazing in person. I'm staying the night at the New Inn and bringing this to the British Museum in the AM. Call me ASAP when you're up.

THE SYMBOLS ON THE SICKLE LOOK LIKE NOTHING YOU'VE EVER SEEN BEFORE.

KLIK

AS SLEEP TAKES YOU, YOU WONDER IF TWIG WILL KNOW WHAT THE SYMBOLS ARE. COULD THEY BE SOME KIND OF LANGUAGE?

BUT IN JUST SECONDS, YOU ARE ASLEEP.

Turn to the next page.

SUDDENLY, YOU AWAKE WITH A JERK.

WHAM!
WHAM!

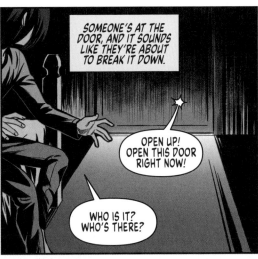

SOMEONE'S AT THE DOOR, AND IT SOUNDS LIKE THEY'RE ABOUT TO BREAK IT DOWN.

OPEN UP! OPEN THIS DOOR RIGHT NOW!

WHO IS IT? WHO'S THERE?

YOU'RE IN POSSESSION OF STOLEN PROPERTY! OPEN THE DOOR AT ONCE!

STOLEN? ARE THEY TALKING ABOUT THE GOLDEN SICKLE?

WHUMP!

THEY'RE THROWING THEMSELVES AGAINST THE DOOR...BUT HOW DID THEY KNOW YOU'RE HERE?

DID SOMEONE SEE ALISTAIR HAND YOU THE SICKLE?

YOU'RE ALMOST POSITIVE NO ONE WAS FOLLOWING WHEN YOU LEFT STONEHENGE, WHICH MEANS...

...SOMEONE MUST HAVE SEEN YOUR TEXT MESSAGE TO TWIG.

If you decide to take the sickle and escape out the window, go on to the next page.

If you decide to call the police on your cell phone, turn to page 23.

I'LL BE RIGHT THERE...JUST PULLING ON MY CLOTHES!

YOU HAVE FIFTEEN SECONDS!

YOU'RE ONLY ON THE SECOND FLOOR...

...SO YOU THINK YOU CAN MAKE A QUICK ESCAPE OUT THE WINDOW.

THERE'S BARELY TIME TO CONSIDER FEELING SCARED.

WHUMP!

WHUMP!

Turn to the next page.

YOU MAKE THE JUMP BEFORE THE INTRUDERS FORCE THEIR WAY INTO THE ROOM.

YOU CAN FEEL PAIN SURGE THROUGH YOUR ARM AS YOU TRY TO BREAK YOUR FALL...

...BUT YOU KNOW YOU NEED TO KEEP MOVING.

YOU THOUGHT ALISTAIR WAS BEING PARANOID WHEN HE SAID SOMEONE MIGHT BE AFTER HIM, AND NOW YOU **WISH** IT WAS JUST PARANOIA.

OI! DOWN THERE!

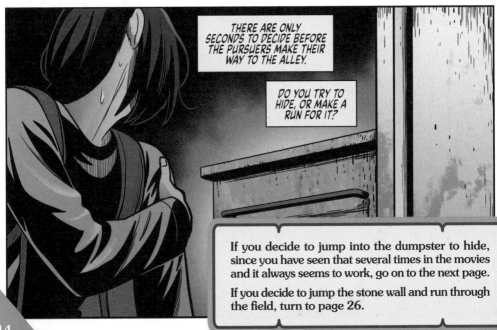

THERE ARE ONLY SECONDS TO DECIDE BEFORE THE PURSUERS MAKE THEIR WAY TO THE ALLEY.

DO YOU TRY TO HIDE, OR MAKE A RUN FOR IT?

If you decide to jump into the dumpster to hide, since you have seen that several times in the movies and it always seems to work, go on to the next page.

If you decide to jump the stone wall and run through the field, turn to page 26.

YOU DECIDE TO JUMP INTO THE DUMPSTER.

IT'S EVEN MORE DISGUSTING THAN YOU IMAGINED, AND THE SMELL HITS YOU ALMOST IMMEDIATELY.

THERE'S NO TIME TO CHANGE YOUR MIND, SO YOU JUMP IN...

...FEELING SOMETHING SQUISHY UNDERNEATH YOU AS YOU LAND.

WHERE'D THEY GO?

THAT BUGGER'S GOTTA BE OUT HERE SOMEWHERE.

HEY...

Turn to the next page.

AFTER A MOMENT YOU JUST HEAR SILENCE. YOU HOPE THEY'VE TAKEN THEIR SEARCH ELSEWHERE.

NO...

'ELLO THERE!

THWAAK!

YOU FEEL A SHARP PAIN IN YOUR SKULL, AND EVERYTHING GOES DARK.

Go on to the next page.

YOU DON'T KNOW HOW LONG YOU'RE INSIDE THE DUMPSTER.

IT HAD TO BE AT LEAST A FEW HOURS...

...BECAUSE THE NEXT THING YOU REMEMBER IS THE SUNLIGHT FILTERING IN.

WHAT...?!

HEY... THERE'S A KID IN HERE!

YOUR HEAD IS SCREAMING, AND IT PAINS YOU TO EVEN TRY TO OPEN YOUR EYES.

CAREFUL THERE...

YOU SQUINT UP AT THE MAN TRYING TO HELP YOU TO YOUR FEET.

WHAT'S YOUR NAME? WHAT HAPPENED HERE?

I...I DON'T REMEMBER. I THINK I HURT MY HEAD.

THEY TAKE YOU TO THE HOSPITAL, BUT IT'S A FULL WEEK BEFORE YOU CAN REMEMBER YOUR NAME.

ALL MEMORIES OF THE PREVIOUS NIGHT, ALONG WITH YOUR BACKPACK AND THE GOLDEN SICKLE, ARE GONE FOREVER...

THE END

17

YOU DECIDE TO WAIT UNTIL MORNING TO TAKE A PICTURE.

TWIG, THE SICKLE, ALISTAIR, STANDISH BLOOM...

...IT CAN ALL WAIT UNTIL THE MORNING.

RIGHT NOW, YOU NEED TO SLEEP.

YOU CAREFULLY PLACE THE SICKLE BACK IN YOUR BAG...

KLIK

...AND WITHIN SECONDS OF YOUR HEAD HITTING THE PILLOW, YOU'RE ENGROSSED IN A DREAM ABOUT STONEHENGE AND FAIRIES.

Go on to the next page.

YOU FEEL RESTED IN THE MORNING, BUT YOUR VIVID DREAMS MAKE YOU FEEL A BIT UNSETTLED.

AT ONE POINT THROUGH THE NIGHT, YOU EVEN THOUGHT YOU MIGHT HAVE HEARD SOMEONE OUTSIDE YOUR DOOR...

...BUT YOU BRUSH IT OFF AS YOUR IMAGINATION.

YOU SEND A PICTURE OF THE SICKLE TO TWIG.

IT LOOKS EVEN MORE GORGEOUS IN THE MORNING LIGHT THAN THE NIGHT BEFORE.

YOU CAN'T WAIT FOR TWIG TO SEE IT.

SUDDENLY, YOU SEE THE TIME AND REALIZE YOU'RE GOING TO BE LATE FOR YOUR TRAIN BACK TO LONDON.

YOU HOPE TWIG CALLS YOU BACK ON YOUR WAY. YOU GRAB THE TOAST AND YOUR BACKPACK...

Turn to the next page.

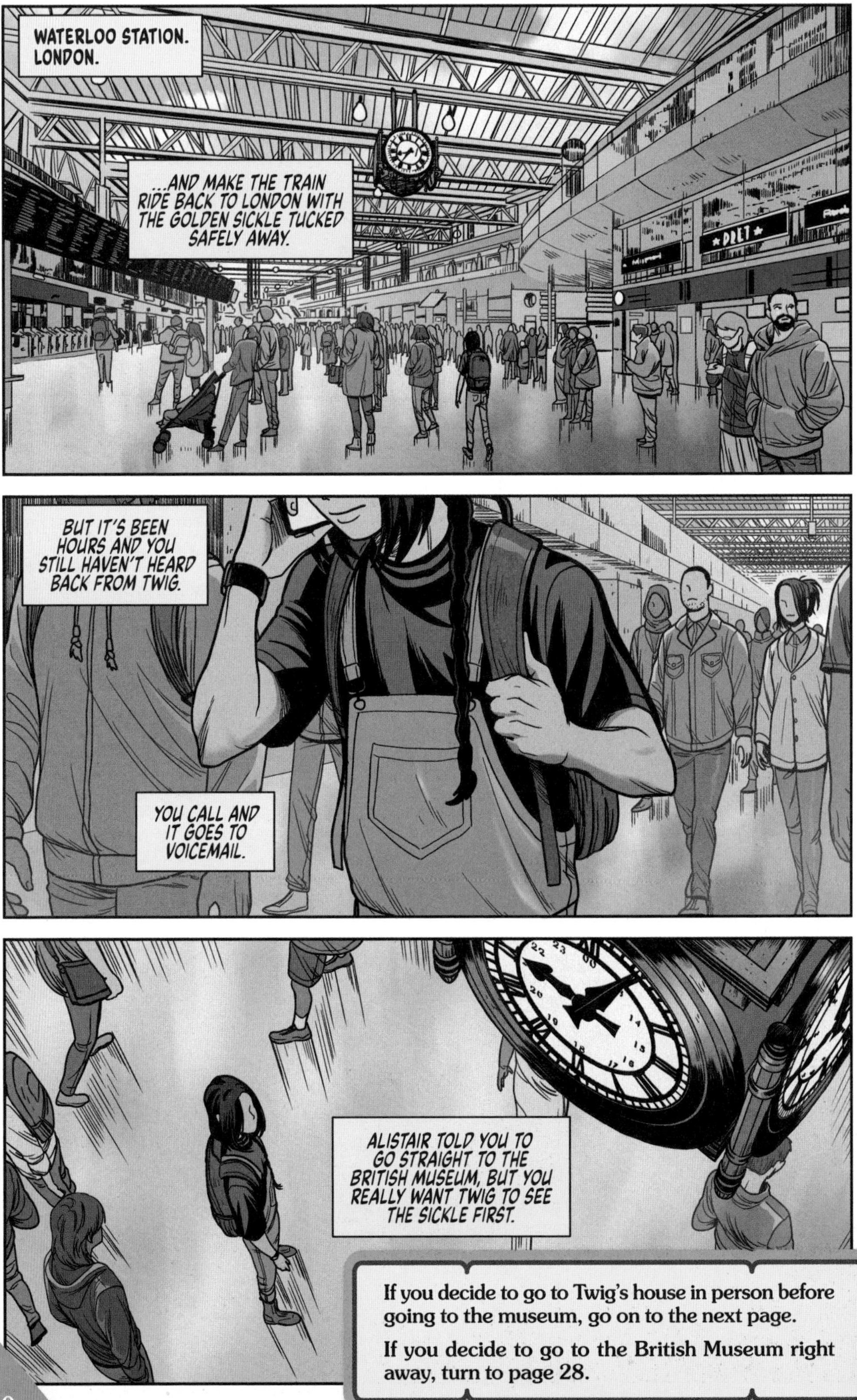
WATERLOO STATION.
LONDON.
...AND MAKE THE TRAIN RIDE BACK TO LONDON WITH THE GOLDEN SICKLE TUCKED SAFELY AWAY.
BUT IT'S BEEN HOURS AND YOU STILL HAVEN'T HEARD BACK FROM TWIG.
YOU CALL AND IT GOES TO VOICEMAIL.
ALISTAIR TOLD YOU TO GO STRAIGHT TO THE BRITISH MUSEUM, BUT YOU REALLY WANT TWIG TO SEE THE SICKLE FIRST.

If you decide to go to Twig's house in person before going to the museum, go on to the next page.

If you decide to go to the British Museum right away, turn to page 28.

YOU DECIDE TO HEAD TO TWIG.

HE'S ALWAYS ON HIS CELL PHONE, AND YOU WANT TO MAKE SURE HE'S ALL RIGHT.

THE RAIN IS COLD, AND THE TAXI LINE IS WRAPPED AROUND THE BUILDING.

BUT YOU HAVE A SPECIAL TECHNIQUE LEARNED FROM YOUR UNCLE BEN.

TWO BLOCKS AWAY, THERE'S A CABSTAND AND HARDLY EVER A WAIT.

WHAT'S A TWO-BLOCK WALK COMPARED TO A TWENTY-MINUTE WAIT?

Turn to the next page.

QUITE A LOT, IT TURNS OUT.

YOU FAILED TO NOTICE THE MAN AND WOMAN WHO FOLLOWED YOU FROM THE STATION.

DID THEY FOLLOW YOU ALL THE WAY FROM AMESBURY?

YOU CAN'T REMEMBER SEEING THEM.

THEY GO IMMEDIATELY FOR YOUR BACKPACK...

...AND JUST FOR GOOD MEASURE, THEY BIND YOUR HANDS AND FEET BEFORE MAKING OFF WITH THE GOLDEN SICKLE.

YOU JUST HOPE SOMEONE FINDS YOU BEFORE THE WEEKEND...

THE END

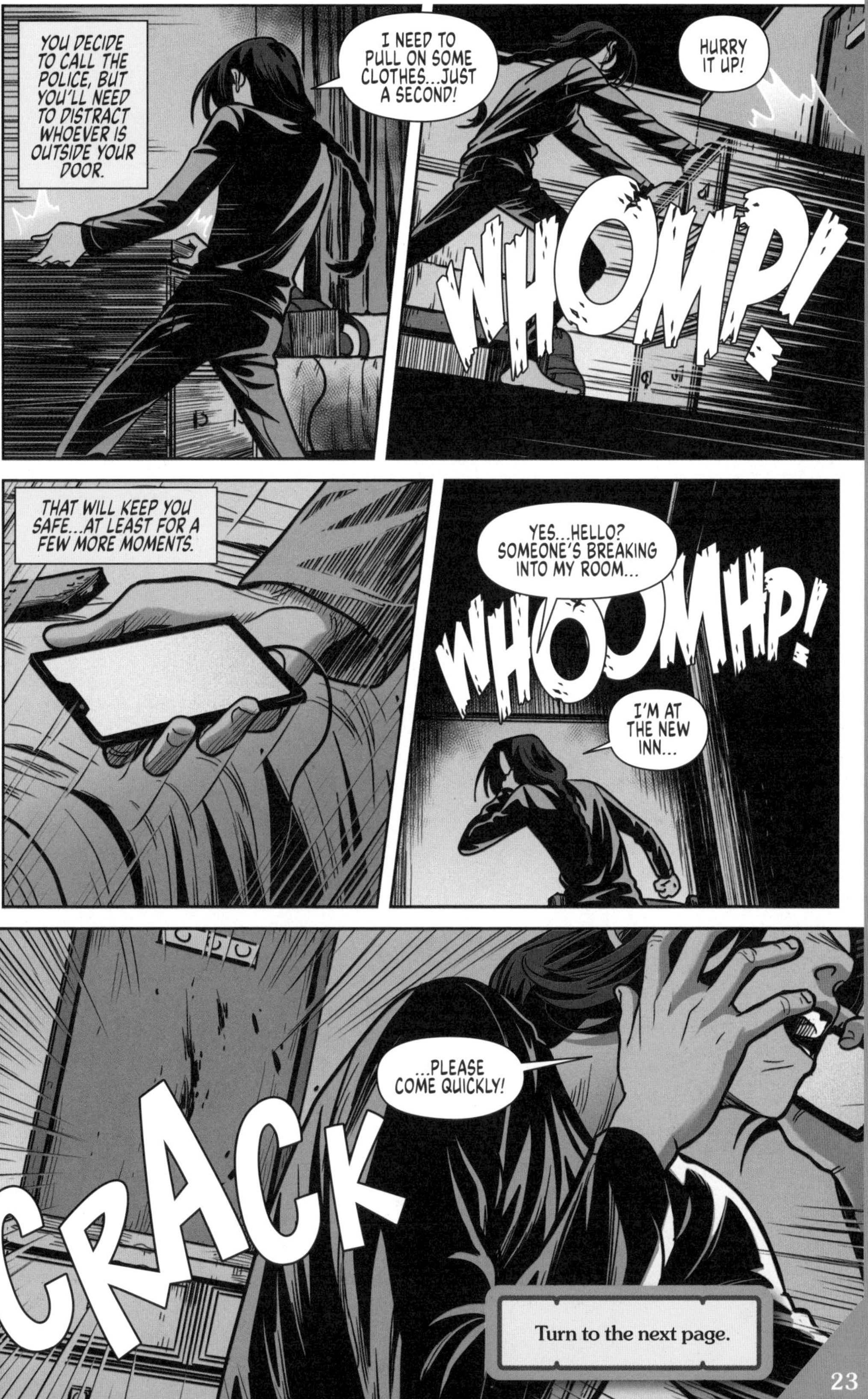
YOU DECIDE TO CALL THE POLICE, BUT YOU'LL NEED TO DISTRACT WHOEVER IS OUTSIDE YOUR DOOR.
I NEED TO PULL ON SOME CLOTHES...JUST A SECOND!
HURRY IT UP!
WHOMP!
THAT WILL KEEP YOU SAFE...AT LEAST FOR A FEW MORE MOMENTS.
YES...HELLO? SOMEONE'S BREAKING INTO MY ROOM...
WHOOMHP!
I'M AT THE NEW INN...
...PLEASE COME QUICKLY!
CRACK
Turn to the next page.

THE DRESSER IS HEAVY AS SOMEONE ON THE OTHER SIDE PUSHES AGAINST THE DOOR.

WHOOMP!

IT FEELS LIKE YOU ARE HOLDING THE DRESSER FOREVER...BUT IT'S PROBABLY ONLY A COUPLE OF MINUTES BEFORE YOU START TO HEAR THE SIRENS.

WHOOMP!

THE BANGING ON THE DOOR SUDDENLY STOPS, AND YOU HEAR A WOMAN'S VOICE CALLING FROM DOWN THE HALL, BUT...IT SOUNDS FAMILIAR...IT SOUNDS LIKE...

WHEEEOOO!

IT'S THE COPS! WE'VE GOT TO RUN. THEY'RE PULLING UP OUTSIDE.

...IT'S ELAINE, THE FAIRY YOU MET AT STONEHENGE!

Go on to the next page.

24

WE'LL GET YOU ONE OF THESE DAYS... THE SICKLE DOESN'T BELONG TO YOU.

YOU CAN FEEL SWEAT ROLLING DOWN THE BACK OF YOUR NECK.

MAYBE ALISTAIR'S PARANOIA WASN'T SO UNFOUNDED AFTER ALL.

BUT THE SICKLE IS SAFE. WHEN THE POLICE ARRIVE, YOU TELL THEM YOUR ENTIRE STORY.

A PLAINCLOTHES DETECTIVE BRINGS YOU BACK TO THE STATION, WHERE YOU'RE ASKED TO RECOUNT THE EVENTS OF THE LAST DAY FROM THE BEGINNING...

THE END

YOU DECIDE TO JUMP THE STONE WALL AND MAKE FOR THE HILL IN THE DISTANCE.

MAYBE YOU CAN HIDE THERE UNTIL MORNING.

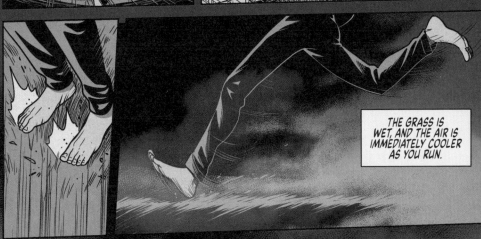

THE GRASS IS WET, AND THE AIR IS IMMEDIATELY COOLER AS YOU RUN.

THE FOG SEEMS TO GET THICKER AS YOU RUN.

Go on to the next page.

SUDDENLY, YOU HAVE TO STOP RUNNING. YOU CAN'T SEE ANYTHING THROUGH THIS FOG... BEHIND OR AHEAD.

THAT'S WHEN YOU HEAR IT...

THE CURSE OF THE GOLDEN SICKLE IS OLD AND DEEP. YOU ARE DOOMED TO RUN IN THE FOG UNTIL NEXT YEAR'S SOLSTICE.

WHO SAID THAT?

BUT YOUR ONLY ANSWER IS THE HOWLING WIND...

THE END

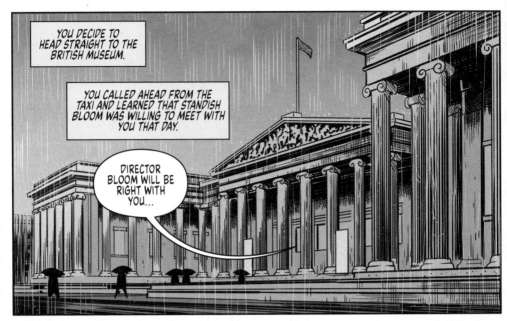

YOU DECIDE TO HEAD STRAIGHT TO THE BRITISH MUSEUM.

YOU CALLED AHEAD FROM THE TAXI AND LEARNED THAT STANDISH BLOOM WAS WILLING TO MEET WITH YOU THAT DAY.

DIRECTOR BLOOM WILL BE RIGHT WITH YOU...

...ARE YOU SURE I CAN'T GET YOU ANYTHING TO DRINK WHILE YOU WAIT?

I'M GOOD. THANK YOU, THOUGH.

YOU HALF EXPECTED DR. BLOOM'S OFFICE TO TURN YOU AWAY...

...OR FOR DR. BLOOM TO NOT BE REAL.

OKAY, THEN. HE'LL BE RIGHT IN.

Go on to the next page.

YOU CAN'T IMAGINE WHAT DR. BLOOM WILL SAY WHEN YOU SHOW HIM THE SICKLE.

WILL YOU FINALLY LEARN WHY ALISTAIR SHEPHERD WAS SO ANXIOUS BACK AT THE HENGE?

LUCKILY, YOU DON'T HAVE TO WAIT LONG...

TAC TAC TAC

DID YOU BRING IT WITH YOU?

DR. BLOOM ENTERS THE ROOM WITHOUT SO MUCH AS AN INTRODUCTION.

YOU'RE TAKEN ABACK BY HIS BRUSQUE AND SUDDEN ENTRANCE.

THE... SICKLE? OF COURSE.

Turn to the next page.

I'M SORRY. MY EXCITEMENT GOT THE BETTER OF ME.

I'M DIRECTOR STANDISH BLOOM...

...BUT PLEASE, JUST CALL ME STANDISH.

SO TELL ME ABOUT IT. HOW DID YOU COME ACROSS THE GOLDEN SICKLE?

LAST NIGHT I HAD A MEETING WITH A MAN NAMED ALISTAIR SHEPHERD. YOU KNOW HIM, CORRECT?

YES, VERY WELL.

I THOUGHT HE WAS GOING TO TELL ME SOMETHING ABOUT THE MISSING HEEL STONE...

I'M A BIT OF AN AMATEUR ARCHEOLOGIST. BUT INSTEAD...

...HE GAVE ME THIS.

Go on to the next page.

AHH...

I'VE DREAMT OF THIS MOMENT FOR A LONG, LONG TIME.

WHAT IS IT, EXACTLY?

THIS MAY BE THE FABLED GOLDEN SICKLE OF THE DUNEDAIN.

THE DRUIDS RECORDED ITS HISTORY.

BUT...I THOUGHT THE DRUIDS DIDN'T WRITE ANYTHING DOWN?

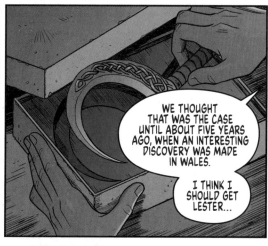

WE THOUGHT THAT WAS THE CASE UNTIL ABOUT FIVE YEARS AGO, WHEN AN INTERESTING DISCOVERY WAS MADE IN WALES.

I THINK I SHOULD GET LESTER...

HE'S THE BEST DATER WE HAVE AND CAN HELP US AUTHENTICATE THE SICKLE.

Turn to the next page.

31

YOUR HEART RACES, AND YOU REALIZE THIS COULD BE BIGGER THAN YOU IMAGINED.

RRRZZZZ!
RRRZZZZ!

YOU THINK TWIG HAS FINALLY SEEN THE PICTURE OF THE SICKLE, AND YOU'RE EXCITED TO GIVE HIM AN UPDATE...

TWIG?

HAVE YOU GIVEN HIM THE SICKLE?

...BUT THE VOICE ON THE OTHER END IS GRUFF AND FRIGHTENED.

ALISTAIR?

WHATEVER YOU DO, DON'T GIVE IT TO HIM! I WAS WRONG TO SEND YOU TO BLOOM...HE'S ONE OF THEM!

ONE OF WHOM? WHAT ARE YOU TALKING ABOUT?

ALISTAIR... I...

HERE WE ARE...

I CAN'T EXPLAIN NOW. YOU HAVE TO GET OUT OF THERE. IMMEDIATELY.

YOUR LIFE IS IN DANGER. DON'T GIVE HIM THE SICKLE OR ALL IS LOST...

Go on to the next page.

...WE WANT TO THANK YOU AGAIN FOR BRINGING US THE SICKLE.

LESTER WILL TAKE IT TO THE LAB TO ANALYZE AND DATE IT. BUT YOU WILL, OF COURSE, GET FULL CREDIT FOR THE WONDERFUL DISCOVERY.

THIS COULD MAKE YOU QUITE FAMOUS, YOU KNOW.

WAIT...

If you choose to follow Alistair's instructions and take the sickle back, turn to the next page.

If you decide to let Dr. Bloom have the sickle, turn to page 39.

I NEVER SAID YOU COULD HAVE THE SICKLE. I JUST WANTED YOU TO EXAMINE IT AND GIVE ME BACKGROUND ON IT.

I'M AFRAID YOU DON'T UNDERSTAND THE REALITY OF THE SITUATION.

WE APPRECIATE THAT YOU HELPED BRING IT TO OUR ATTENTION, BUT ALL ANTIQUITIES FOUND IN THE UNITED KINGDOM ARE PROPERTY OF THE CROWN.

IT'S ILLEGAL TO HOLD THEM PERSONALLY.

HOW DO YOU KNOW THIS IS FROM THE UK? NOTHING I'VE SEEN HAS GIVEN ME ANY PROOF TO THAT EFFECT.

DON'T BE FOOLISH...

THE INSINCERE SMILE PLASTERED ON BLOOM'S FACE MAKES YOU GLAD YOU DIDN'T GIVE HIM THE SICKLE.

DON'T MAKE US CALL SECURITY. JUST HAND OVER THE BOX, AND WE'LL FORGET THIS BIT OF UNPLEASANTNESS.

Go on to the next page.

34

SURE, I'LL GIVE IT TO YOU AS SOON AS YOU RETURN THE ELGIN MARBLES!

STOP!

COME BACK HERE!

Turn to the next page.

YOU DON'T KNOW WHERE YOU'RE GOING TO GO, BUT YOU KNOW YOU NEED TO GET OUT OF THE MUSEUM.

ALISTAIR JUST TOLD YOU TO RUN, BUT HE DIDN'T SAY WHERE TO RUN TO.

AROOOO!

AS YOU CONSIDER CALLING TWIG, YOU REALIZE YOU LEFT YOUR BACKPACK IN DR. BLOOM'S OFFICE.

Go on to the next page.

NOTHING IRREPLACEABLE IN THE BAG. LUCKILY, YOUR PHONE AND WALLET ARE IN YOUR JACKET POCKET.

BUT THEY'LL LEARN YOUR HOME ADDRESS. ONE LESS PLACE YOU CAN NOW GO TO HIDE.

CALLING TWIG MIGHT NOT BE SMART EITHER. WHAT IF THEY CAN TRACK YOUR CELL PHONE?

NO SIGN OF BLOOM OR HIS SIDEKICK. GOOD.

Turn to the next page.

YOU RIDE THE LONDON UNDERGROUND RANDOMLY FOR AN HOUR, CHANGING TRAINS FREQUENTLY.

NO ONE SEEMS TO BE ON YOUR TRAIL.

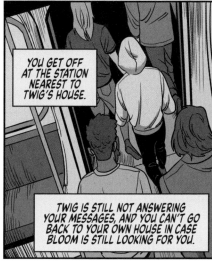

YOU GET OFF AT THE STATION NEAREST TO TWIG'S HOUSE.

TWIG IS STILL NOT ANSWERING YOUR MESSAGES, AND YOU CAN'T GO BACK TO YOUR OWN HOUSE IN CASE BLOOM IS STILL LOOKING FOR YOU.

BUT AS YOU LEAVE THE TRAIN, YOUR CELL PHONE BEEPS WITH AN ODD MESSAGE.

DING!

Come to North Yorkshire ASAP. Train from King's Cross at 12:10. See map below. Bring the package I gave you. Don't tell anyone your plans. Will explain when we meet. –Alistair

IT'S 11:40 NOW. YOU HAVE JUST ENOUGH TIME TO CATCH THE TRAIN FROM WATERLOO STATION IF YOU LEAVE IMMEDIATELY.

ASD
CVBNM
space
return

If you decide to try to catch the 12:10 to Yorkshire and call Twig from the train, turn to page 41.

If you decide to go to Twig's first, turn to page 46.

SOMETHING ABOUT THE CALL FROM ALISTAIR DOESN'T SIT RIGHT WITH YOU.

YOU DECIDE TO GIVE THE GOLDEN SICKLE TO DR. BLOOM.

IT MUST BE SAFE IN THE CARE OF A MUSEUM, RIGHT?

THANK YOU SO MUCH FOR COMING BY.

NOW IF YOU'LL EXCUSE US, WE'RE ACTUALLY DUE AT ANOTHER MEETING.

BUT WHAT IF I HAVE QUESTIONS ABOUT--?

WE'LL BE IN TOUCH SHORTLY ONCE WE HAVE VERIFIED DATES.

"I'LL BE KEEN TO SEE WHAT THE MUSEUM HAS TO SAY..."

Turn to the next page.

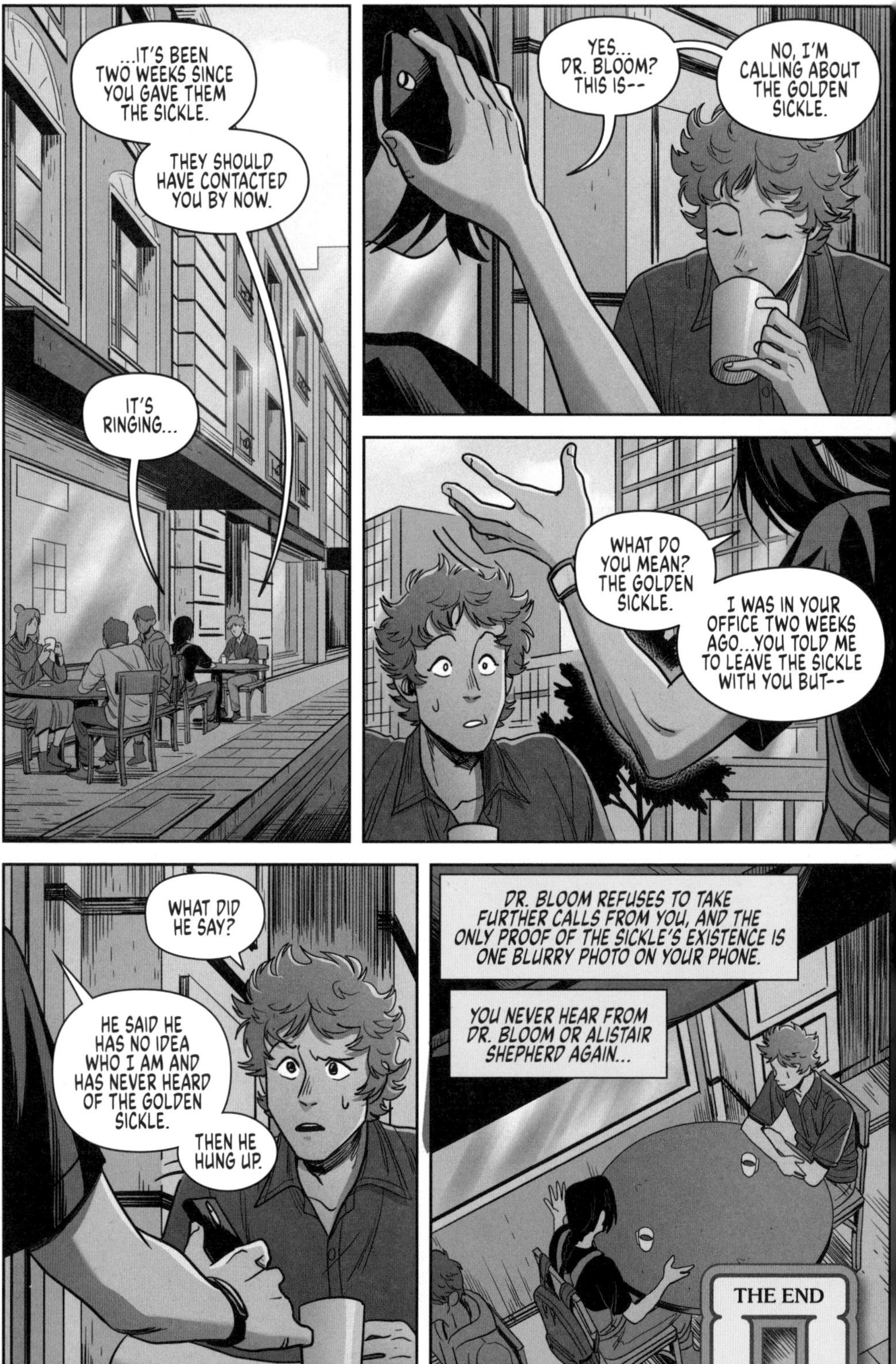
...IT'S BEEN TWO WEEKS SINCE YOU GAVE THEM THE SICKLE.
THEY SHOULD HAVE CONTACTED YOU BY NOW.
IT'S RINGING...
YES... DR. BLOOM? THIS IS--
NO, I'M CALLING ABOUT THE GOLDEN SICKLE.
WHAT DO YOU MEAN? THE GOLDEN SICKLE.
I WAS IN YOUR OFFICE TWO WEEKS AGO...YOU TOLD ME TO LEAVE THE SICKLE WITH YOU BUT--
WHAT DID HE SAY?
HE SAID HE HAS NO IDEA WHO I AM AND HAS NEVER HEARD OF THE GOLDEN SICKLE.
THEN HE HUNG UP.
DR. BLOOM REFUSES TO TAKE FURTHER CALLS FROM YOU, AND THE ONLY PROOF OF THE SICKLE'S EXISTENCE IS ONE BLURRY PHOTO ON YOUR PHONE.
YOU NEVER HEAR FROM DR. BLOOM OR ALISTAIR SHEPHERD AGAIN...
THE END

YOU MAKE AN IMPULSIVE DECISION TO TRY TO CATCH THE TRAIN AND REACH KING'S CROSS STATION WITH ONLY FIVE MINUTES TO SPARE.

YOU TAKE A CAB FROM THE STATION TO THE START OF A TRAILHEAD THAT ALISTAIR MARKED ON THE MAP HE SENT YOU.

DESPITE FEELING DISTRACTED BY ALISTAIR'S WARNING ABOUT BLOOM, YOU DO ENJOY THE VIEW.

Turn to the next page.

A GENTLE BREEZE COOLS YOU AS YOU HIKE.

ALISTAIR'S MAP LEADS TO A LARGE ROCK FORMATION CALLED "WAINSTONES."

THE WAINSTONES ARE A HAPHAZARD JUMBLE OF SANDSTONE BOULDERS, AND YOU LOOK AROUND FOR ALISTAIR AS YOU APPROACH.

BUT AS YOU MOVE BETWEEN TWO LARGE ROCKS...

ALISTAIR?

WHAK!

...SOMETHING HARD SMASHES AGAINST YOUR HEAD, AND EVERYTHING GOES DARK.

Go on to the next page.

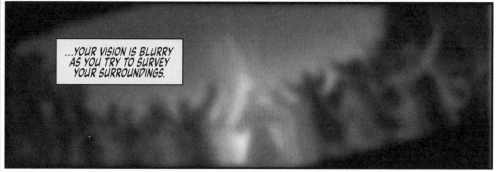

AS YOU COME TO, YOU FEEL A SHARP PAIN SHOOT DOWN YOUR NECK...

...YOUR VISION IS BLURRY AS YOU TRY TO SURVEY YOUR SURROUNDINGS.

YOUR HANDS AND FEET ARE TIED WITH THICK ROPE.

THE SHADOWS OF YOUR PRESUMED CAPTORS DANCE AROUND WHAT LOOKS LIKE A DENSE FOREST.

ONE HOLDS THE SICKLE ABOVE HIS HEAD, AND IT SOUNDS LIKE THEY MIGHT BE CHANTING...BUT YOU CAN'T MAKE OUT WHAT THEY'RE SAYING.

I'M SO SORRY I BROUGHT YOU INTO THIS...

Turn to the next page.

...I HAVE MANAGED TO MAKE A MESS OF THIS WHOLE THING.

ALISTAIR? WHY SHOULD I TALK TO YOU?

THEY MADE ME CALL YOU. I DIDN'T WANT TO DO IT, BUT THEY HAVE WAYS--METHODS--TO MAKE YOU DO THINGS AGAINST YOUR WILL.

I THINK THEY MEAN TO SACRIFICE US TO THE GODS OF THE GREEN AND THE GODS OF THE SUN.

AGAIN... I AM SORRY.

YOU'RE BARELY LISTENING TO WHAT ALISTAIR IS SAYING. YOU'RE MORE FOCUSED ON THE SMALL POCKET KNIFE CLIPPED TO YOUR BELT.

GETTING IT WITHOUT BEING NOTICED IS YOUR MAIN ISSUE.

THEY ARE COMING TO THE END OF THE FIRST PART.

YOU MANAGE TO GET THE KNIFE INTO YOUR BOUND HANDS, BUT IT SOUNDS LIKE YOU'RE RUNNING OUT OF TIME.

THEY WILL ALL TURN AND BOW TO THE ARCH-DRUID. THAT WILL BE YOUR CHANCE TO RUN.

Go on to the next page.

ONCE YOU START RUNNING, I'LL SCREAM AND ROLL INTO THE FIRE. THAT SHOULD DISTRACT THEM LONG ENOUGH FOR YOU TO GET AWAY.

JUST HEAD DOWN THE SLOPE. WE ARE ONLY A COUPLE OF MILES FROM THE TOWN, AND THERE ARE LOTS OF PATHS.

YOU DON'T KNOW WHAT TO MAKE OF ALISTAIR'S PLAN, BUT BEFORE YOU CAN CONSIDER IT...

...YOU SEE THE DRUIDS KNEEL, JUST LIKE ALISTAIR PROMISED.

YOU FEEL THE BINDINGS FALL AWAY AND KNOW THAT THIS IS YOUR CHANCE TO ESCAPE TO FREEDOM.

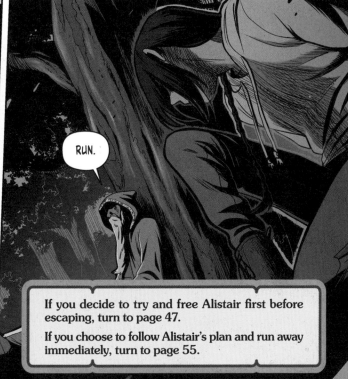

RUN.

If you decide to try and free Alistair first before escaping, turn to page 47.

If you choose to follow Alistair's plan and run away immediately, turn to page 55.

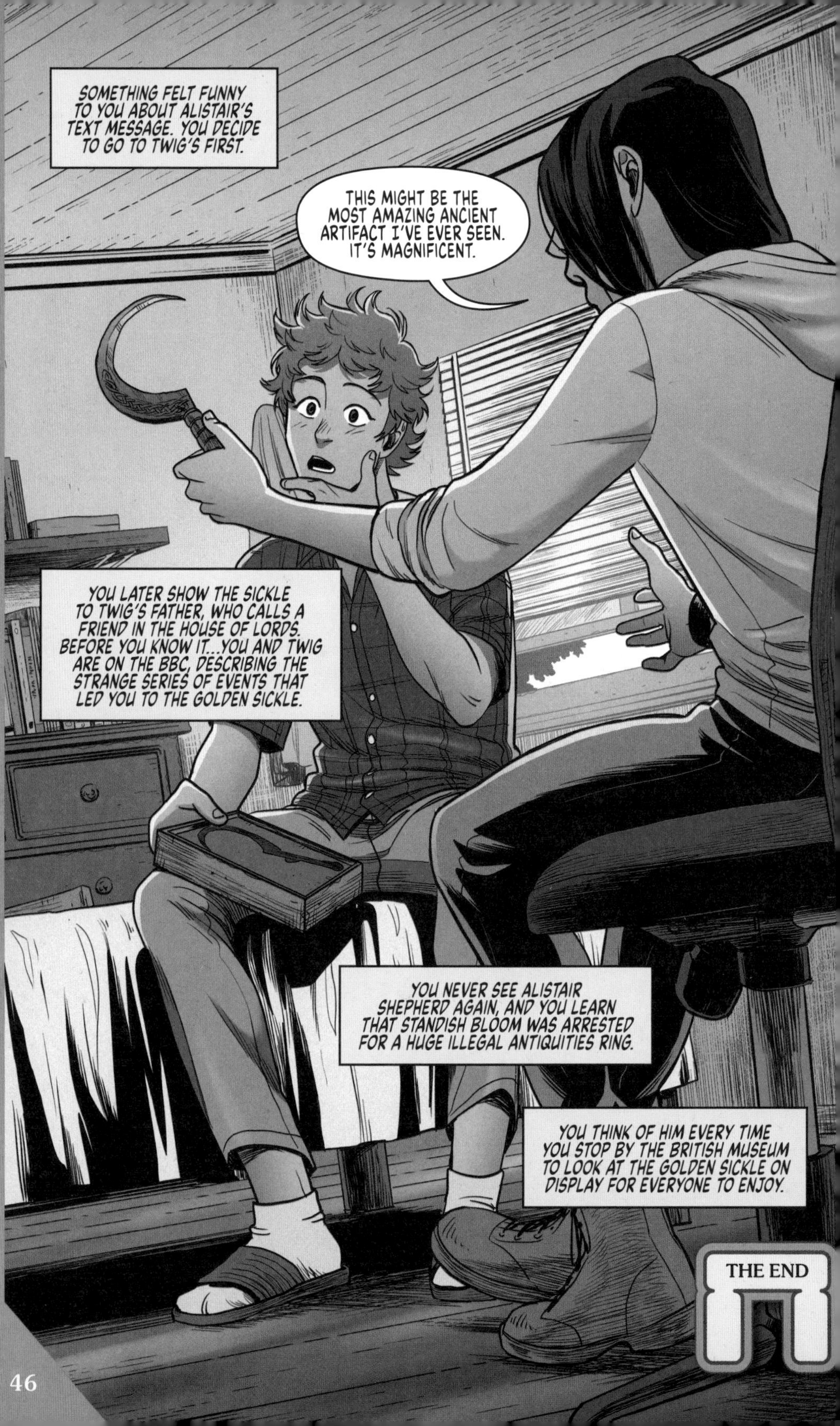
SOMETHING FELT FUNNY TO YOU ABOUT ALISTAIR'S TEXT MESSAGE. YOU DECIDE TO GO TO TWIG'S FIRST.
THIS MIGHT BE THE MOST AMAZING ANCIENT ARTIFACT I'VE EVER SEEN. IT'S MAGNIFICENT.
YOU LATER SHOW THE SICKLE TO TWIG'S FATHER, WHO CALLS A FRIEND IN THE HOUSE OF LORDS. BEFORE YOU KNOW IT...YOU AND TWIG ARE ON THE BBC, DESCRIBING THE STRANGE SERIES OF EVENTS THAT LED YOU TO THE GOLDEN SICKLE.
YOU NEVER SEE ALISTAIR SHEPHERD AGAIN, AND YOU LEARN THAT STANDISH BLOOM WAS ARRESTED FOR A HUGE ILLEGAL ANTIQUITIES RING.
YOU THINK OF HIM EVERY TIME YOU STOP BY THE BRITISH MUSEUM TO LOOK AT THE GOLDEN SICKLE ON DISPLAY FOR EVERYONE TO ENJOY.
THE END

IT'S A TOUGH CHOICE, BUT YOU DECIDE TO TRY TO HELP ALISTAIR ESCAPE. YOU AREN'T SURE THERE'S TIME TO GET TO TOWN AND BACK WITH POLICE BEFORE THE DRUIDS DO SOMETHING TERRIBLE.

PLEASE... JUST GET OUT OF HERE.

MY LIFE IS FORFEIT. THEY WILL TRACK ME DOWN NO MATTER WHERE I GO.

BUT YOU... YOU THEY DON'T CARE ABOUT.

YOU IGNORE HIM AND CONCENTRATE ON SAWING THE CORDS.

THEY'RE FINISHING!

COME ON... NO ONE HAS NOTICED US YET.

Turn to the next page.

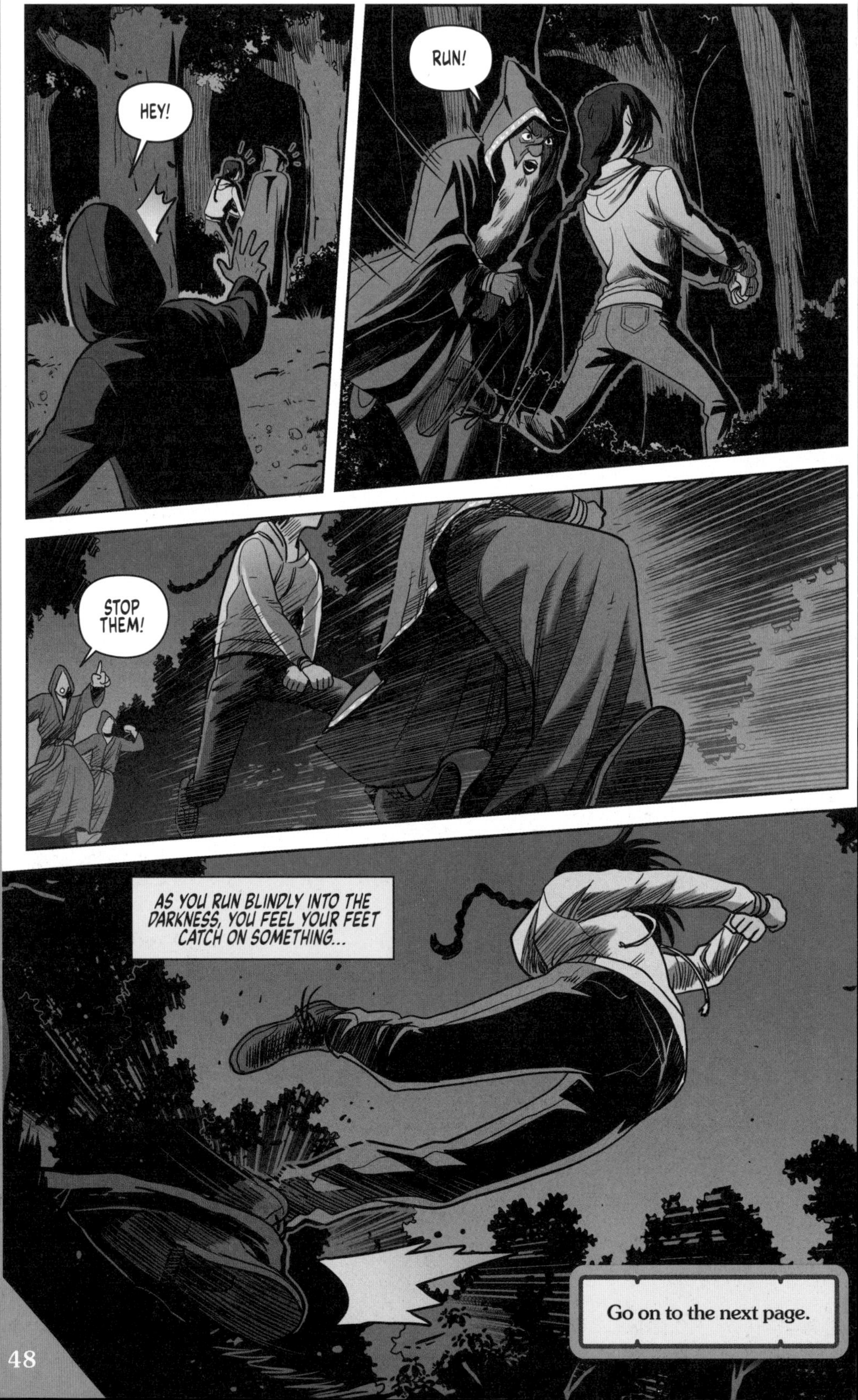
HEY!
RUN!
STOP THEM!
AS YOU RUN BLINDLY INTO THE DARKNESS, YOU FEEL YOUR FEET CATCH ON SOMETHING...
Go on to the next page.

WITH YOUR HANDS STILL BOUND, YOU CAN'T STOP YOUR FALL AND SLIP DOWN A STEEP INCLINE.

YOU ROLL TO A STOP BY WHAT LOOKS LIKE A FARMING PATH OR LOGGING ROAD, BUT THAT WOULD BE TOO OBVIOUS.

INSTEAD, YOU RUN INTO THE THICKEST PART OF THE WOODS, TRYING TO DISTANCE YOURSELF FROM THE DRUIDS.

YOU'VE LOST TRACK OF ALISTAIR IN THE DARKNESS. THERE'S NOTHING MORE YOU COULD DO FOR HIM.

YOU JUST KEEP MOVING AND HOPE THAT THE NOISE OF ALL THE OTHERS WILL MASK YOUR OWN.

HERE!

Turn to the next page.

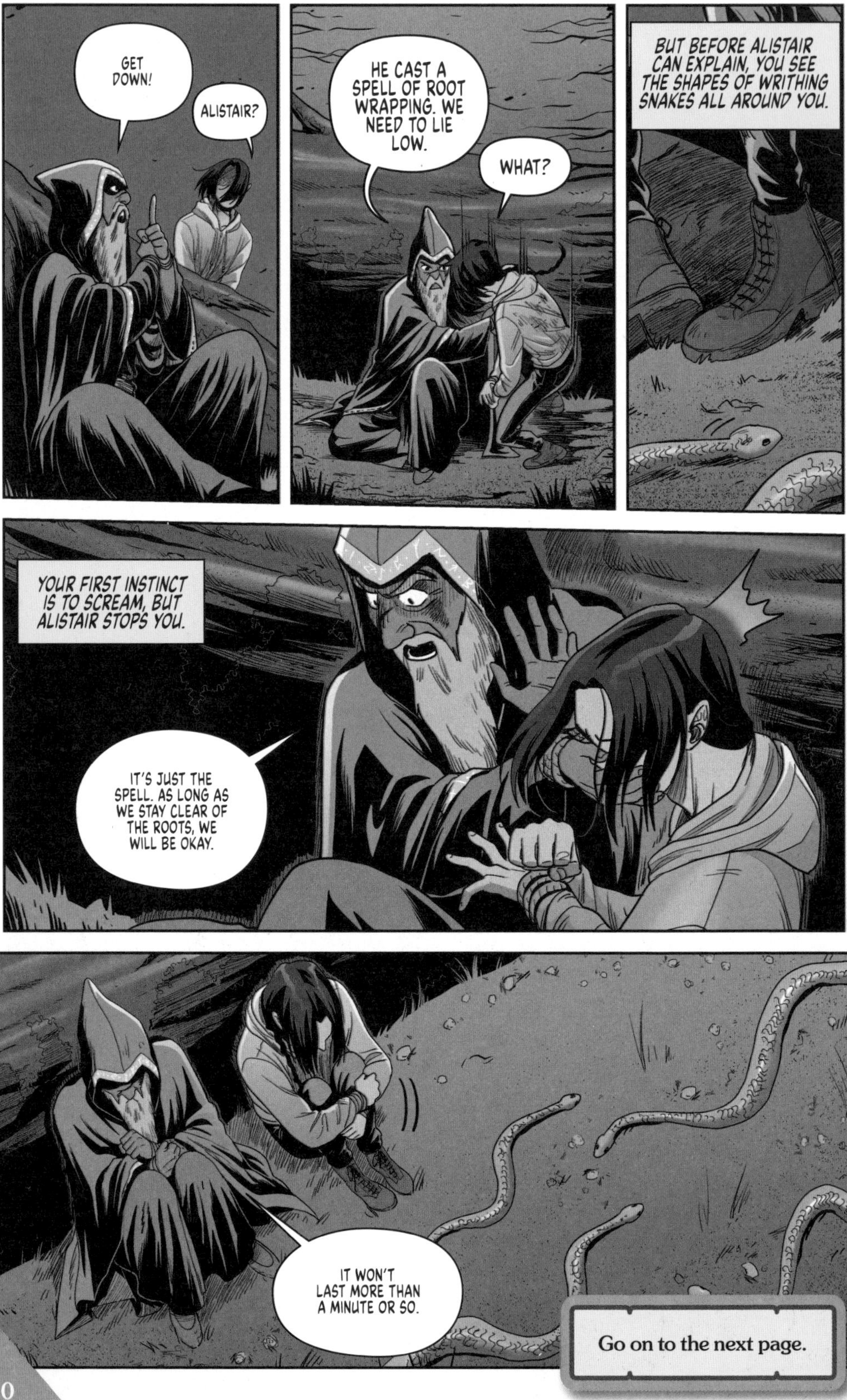
GET DOWN!
ALISTAIR?
HE CAST A SPELL OF ROOT WRAPPING. WE NEED TO LIE LOW.
WHAT?
BUT BEFORE ALISTAIR CAN EXPLAIN, YOU SEE THE SHAPES OF WRITHING SNAKES ALL AROUND YOU.
YOUR FIRST INSTINCT IS TO SCREAM, BUT ALISTAIR STOPS YOU.
IT'S JUST THE SPELL. AS LONG AS WE STAY CLEAR OF THE ROOTS, WE WILL BE OKAY.
IT WON'T LAST MORE THAN A MINUTE OR SO.

Go on to the next page.

YOUR HEART IS POUNDING IN YOUR CHEST, AND YOU TRY TO KEEP FROM SHOUTING.

SSSSSS

INSTINCT KICKS IN AS ONE OF THE SNAKES COMES TOWARD YOUR LEG.

BUT THE OTHER ROOTS SEEM TO FEEL IT. THEY SHAKE LOOSE FROM THE BINDS OF THE EARTH AND BEGIN COMING AT YOU.

SSSSSS

TIME TO GET OUT OF HERE!

SPLSHH!

Turn to the next page.

51

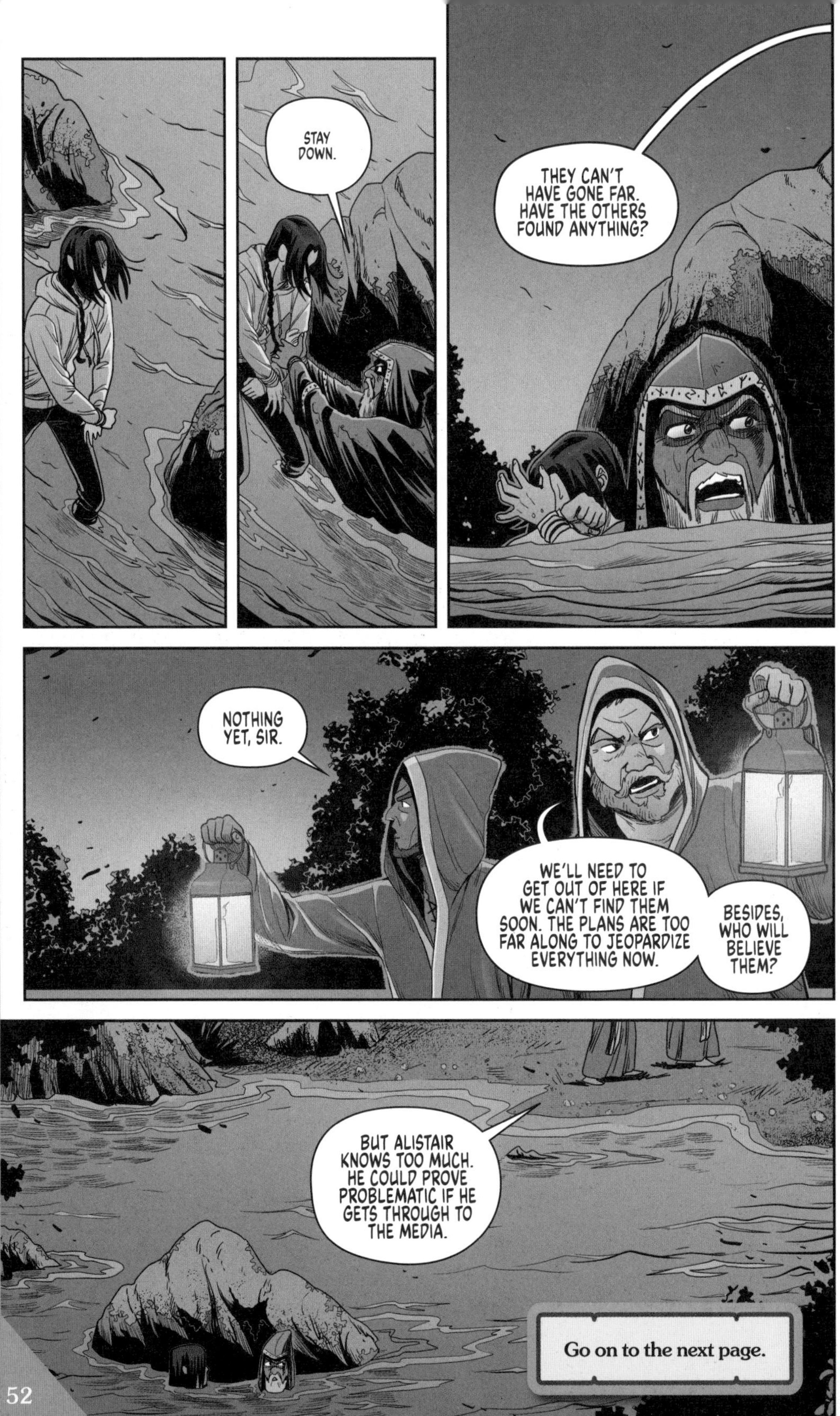
STAY DOWN.
THEY CAN'T HAVE GONE FAR. HAVE THE OTHERS FOUND ANYTHING?
NOTHING YET, SIR.
WE'LL NEED TO GET OUT OF HERE IF WE CAN'T FIND THEM SOON. THE PLANS ARE TOO FAR ALONG TO JEOPARDIZE EVERYTHING NOW.
BESIDES, WHO WILL BELIEVE THEM?
BUT ALISTAIR KNOWS TOO MUCH. HE COULD PROVE PROBLEMATIC IF HE GETS THROUGH TO THE MEDIA.

Go on to the next page.

YOU'RE RIGHT. WE NEED TO FIND THEM.

IF WE DON'T CALL EVERYONE BACK TO THE STONES...

"...WE'LL PERFORM THE DEATH SPELL ONCE WE GET TO THE GROVE."

ALISTAIR SHALL FIND THAT LEAVING THE SUNS IS NOT AS EASY AS HE WOULD LIKE TO THINK.

LET'S KEEP MOVING.

WHAT IS THE DEATH SPELL?

WHEN YOU BECOME ONE OF THE INNER CIRCLE OF THE SUNS OF STONEHENGE, YOU ARE BOUND, BOTH LITERALLY AND FIGURATIVELY, TO THE SACRED GROVE.

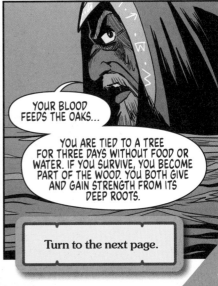

YOUR BLOOD FEEDS THE OAKS...

YOU ARE TIED TO A TREE FOR THREE DAYS WITHOUT FOOD OR WATER. IF YOU SURVIVE, YOU BECOME PART OF THE WOOD. YOU BOTH GIVE AND GAIN STRENGTH FROM ITS DEEP ROOTS.

Turn to the next page.

If you decide to join Alistair on his journey to the wood sprite, turn to page 61.

If you choose to go to the police station and bring Alistair with you, turn to page 71.

54

I'LL BE BACK FOR YOU.

YOU DECIDE TO TRY AND FIND HELP.

AS YOU RUN INTO THE FOREST, THE LIGHT BEGINS TO DISAPPEAR.

YOU HEAR SCREAMING FROM BEHIND YOU, BUT YOU DON'T DARE STOP OR TURN AROUND.

AIIIEEEEE!

GETTING OUT OF THE FOREST IS YOUR ONLY CHANCE TO HELP ALISTAIR.

BUT IN THE DARKNESS, YOU CAN BARELY SEE ONE STEP AHEAD OF YOU...

Turn to the next page.

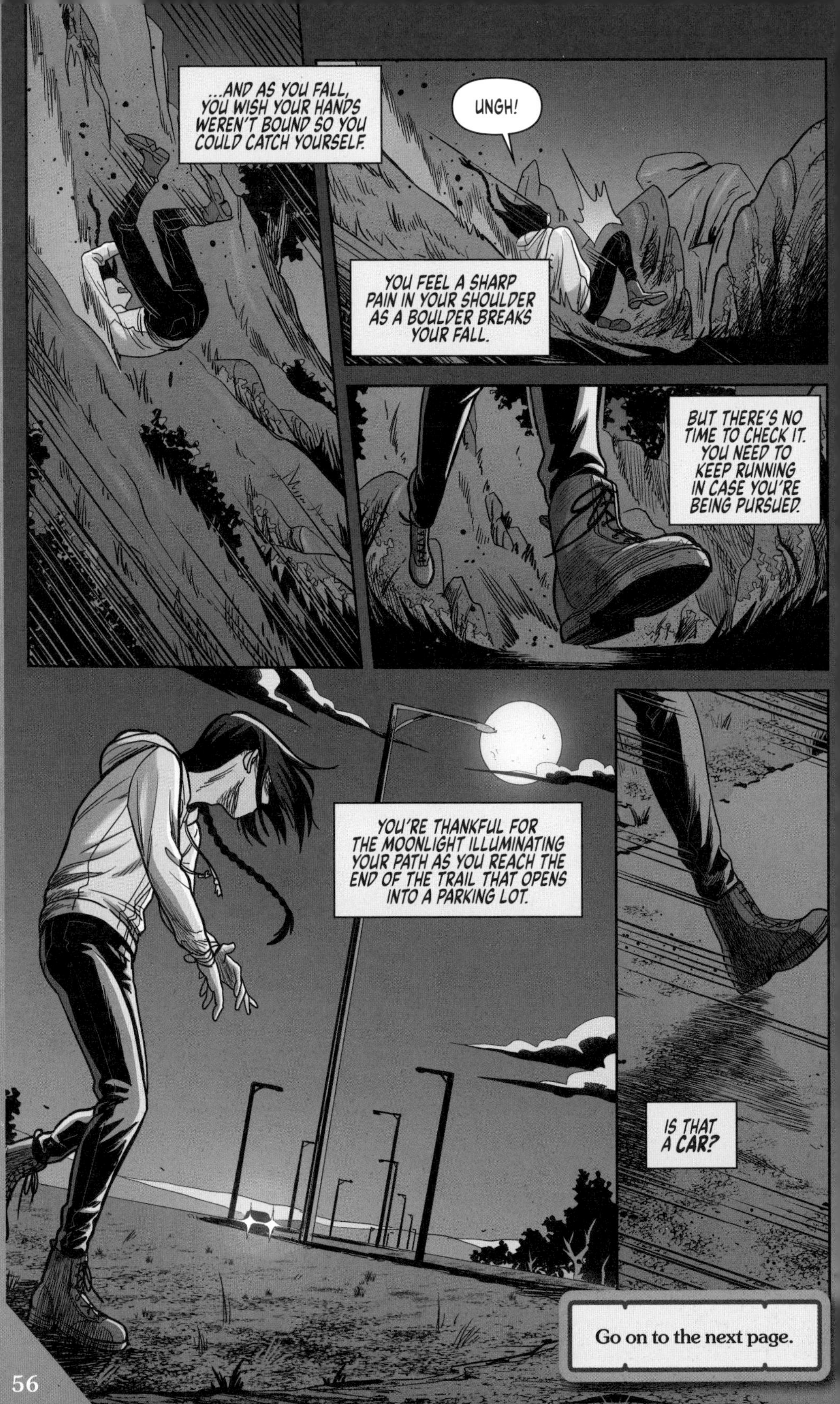
...AND AS YOU FALL, YOU WISH YOUR HANDS WEREN'T BOUND SO YOU COULD CATCH YOURSELF.
UNGH!
YOU FEEL A SHARP PAIN IN YOUR SHOULDER AS A BOULDER BREAKS YOUR FALL.
BUT THERE'S NO TIME TO CHECK IT. YOU NEED TO KEEP RUNNING IN CASE YOU'RE BEING PURSUED.
YOU'RE THANKFUL FOR THE MOONLIGHT ILLUMINATING YOUR PATH AS YOU REACH THE END OF THE TRAIL THAT OPENS INTO A PARKING LOT.
IS THAT A CAR?

Go on to the next page.

WITHOUT THINKING, YOU RUN RIGHT INTO THE MIDDLE OF THE ROAD.

SCREEEEEEEEEE

THE DRIVER TAKES YOU STRAIGHT TO THE POLICE STATION, WHERE THEY AGREE TO SEND A TEAM TO CHECK YOUR STORY...

Turn to the next page.

...BUT AS YOU FEARED, THERE IS NO SIGN OF ANYTHING IN THE FOREST OR AT THE WAINSTONES.

THE POLICE TAKE PICTURES OF THE SCENE AND COLLECT MUD SAMPLES FOR TESTING, BUT THERE IS NOT MUCH MORE THAT THEY CAN DO.

Go on to the next page.

AFTER SPENDING A LONG NIGHT IN THE POLICE STATION TALKING TO DETECTIVES AND PROVIDING STATEMENTS, YOU BEGIN TO BELIEVE THAT THE POLICE WON'T FIND ANY TRACES OF ALISTAIR OR THE DRUIDS.

SORRY TO INTERRUPT, SIR... BUT WE'VE FOUND SOMETHING...

WELL, SOMEONE. WE FOUND SOMEONE MATCHING THE DESCRIPTION OF ONE ALISTAIR SHEPHERD WALKING ALONG THE CLIFFS NEAR THE NORTH SEA.

LET ME SEE HIM.

YES, LET'S SEE HIM. WE WILL NEED TO POSITIVELY IDENTIFY HIM.

Turn to the next page.

TWO FLAPJACKS IN THE MORNING. RIGHT AS RAIN. RAIN OR SHINE. TWO. ALWAYS TWO. OR NO GOOD FOR YOU!

ALISTAIR, IT'S ME. DO YOU RECOGNIZE ME?

FRIAR TUCK ALWAYS ATE SIX. ROBIN DIDN'T LIKE THAT, BUT MAID MARIAN TOOK PITY ON THE HOLY MAN AND WOULD GIVE HIM A COUPLE EXTRA.

SOMETHING HAS OBVIOUSLY HAPPENED TO HIM. HE'LL NEED SOME SORT OF HELP.

SHALL I CALL A CAB FOR YOU TO TAKE HIM HOME?

YOU REALIZE YOU HAVE NO IDEA WHERE ALISTAIR LIVES. WHEN YOU FINALLY REACH TWIG, YOU DISCOVER THAT NEITHER DOES HE.

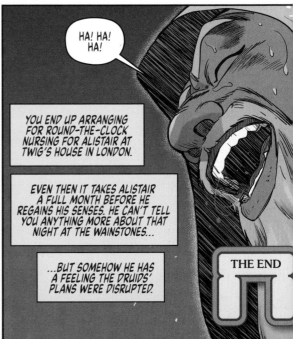

HA! HA! HA!

YOU END UP ARRANGING FOR ROUND-THE-CLOCK NURSING FOR ALISTAIR AT TWIG'S HOUSE IN LONDON.

EVEN THEN IT TAKES ALISTAIR A FULL MONTH BEFORE HE REGAINS HIS SENSES. HE CAN'T TELL YOU ANYTHING MORE ABOUT THAT NIGHT AT THE WAINSTONES...

...BUT SOMEHOW HE HAS A FEELING THE DRUIDS' PLANS WERE DISRUPTED.

THE END

YOU AND ALISTAIR CALL A CAB FROM THE TOWN AND MAKE YOUR WAY NORTH.

THE RIDE TAKES ABOUT AN HOUR, AND THE CABBIE DROPS YOU BY THE EDGE OF A DARK FOREST, WHERE YOU FOLLOW ALISTAIR TOWARD A CLEARING.

THIS IS ONE OF THE OLDEST WOODS IN BRITAIN. MOST OF ALL THE TREES IN ENGLAND HAVE BEEN CUT DOWN, EITHER DURING WARS OR THE INDUSTRIAL REVOLUTION.

THIS IS ONE OF THE FEW SPOTS THAT SURVIVED ALL THAT. I CAME HERE OFTEN AS A YOUNG MAN. THAT IS WHEN I MET LIANDRA.

THE WOODS AROUND YOU HAVE A PROFOUNDLY PEACEFUL FEELING. A WELCOME RELIEF AFTER YOUR FLIGHT FROM THE DRUIDS.

Turn to the next page.

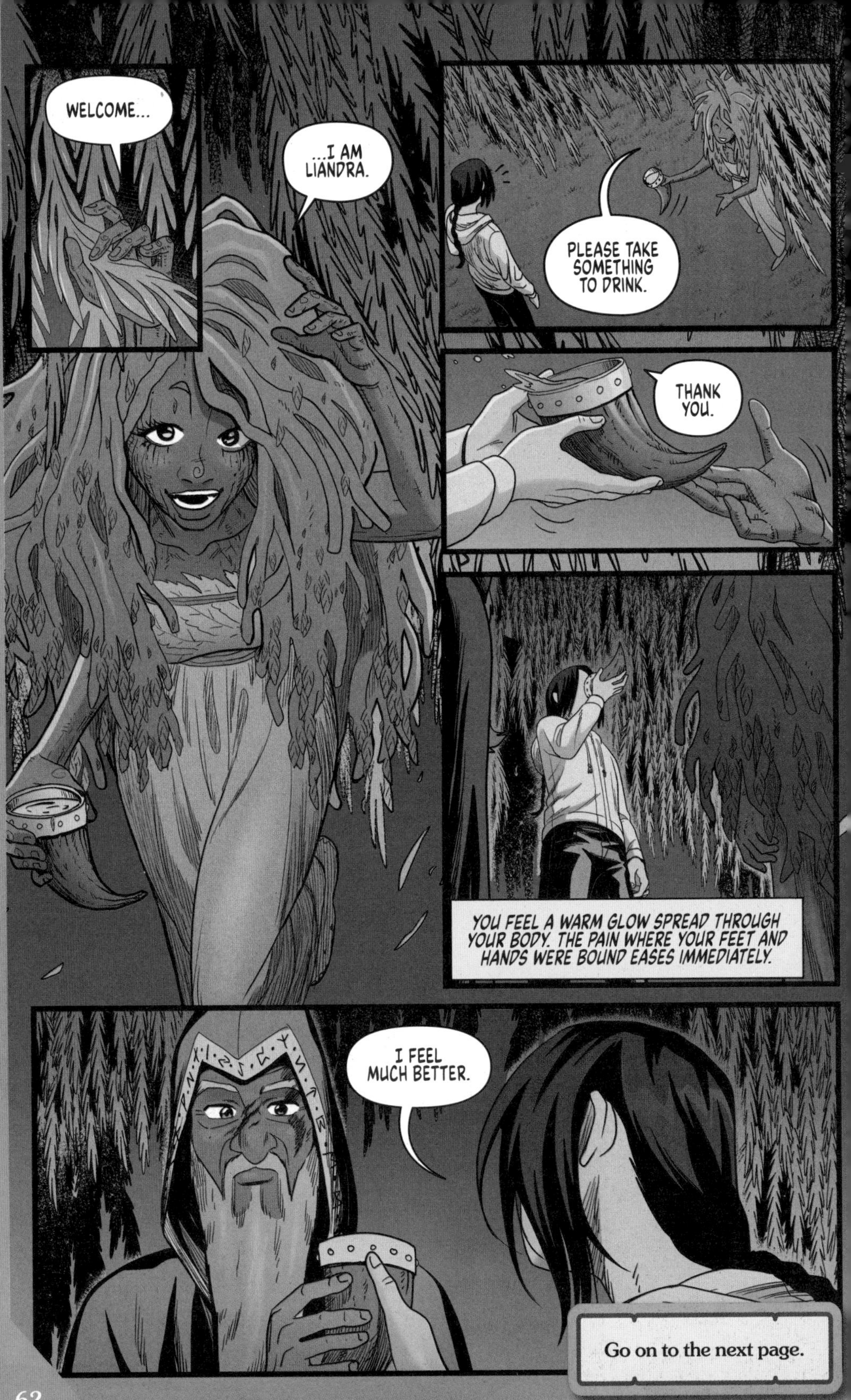
WELCOME...
...I AM LIANDRA.
PLEASE TAKE SOMETHING TO DRINK.
THANK YOU.
YOU FEEL A WARM GLOW SPREAD THROUGH YOUR BODY. THE PAIN WHERE YOUR FEET AND HANDS WERE BOUND EASES IMMEDIATELY.
I FEEL MUCH BETTER.
Go on to the next page.

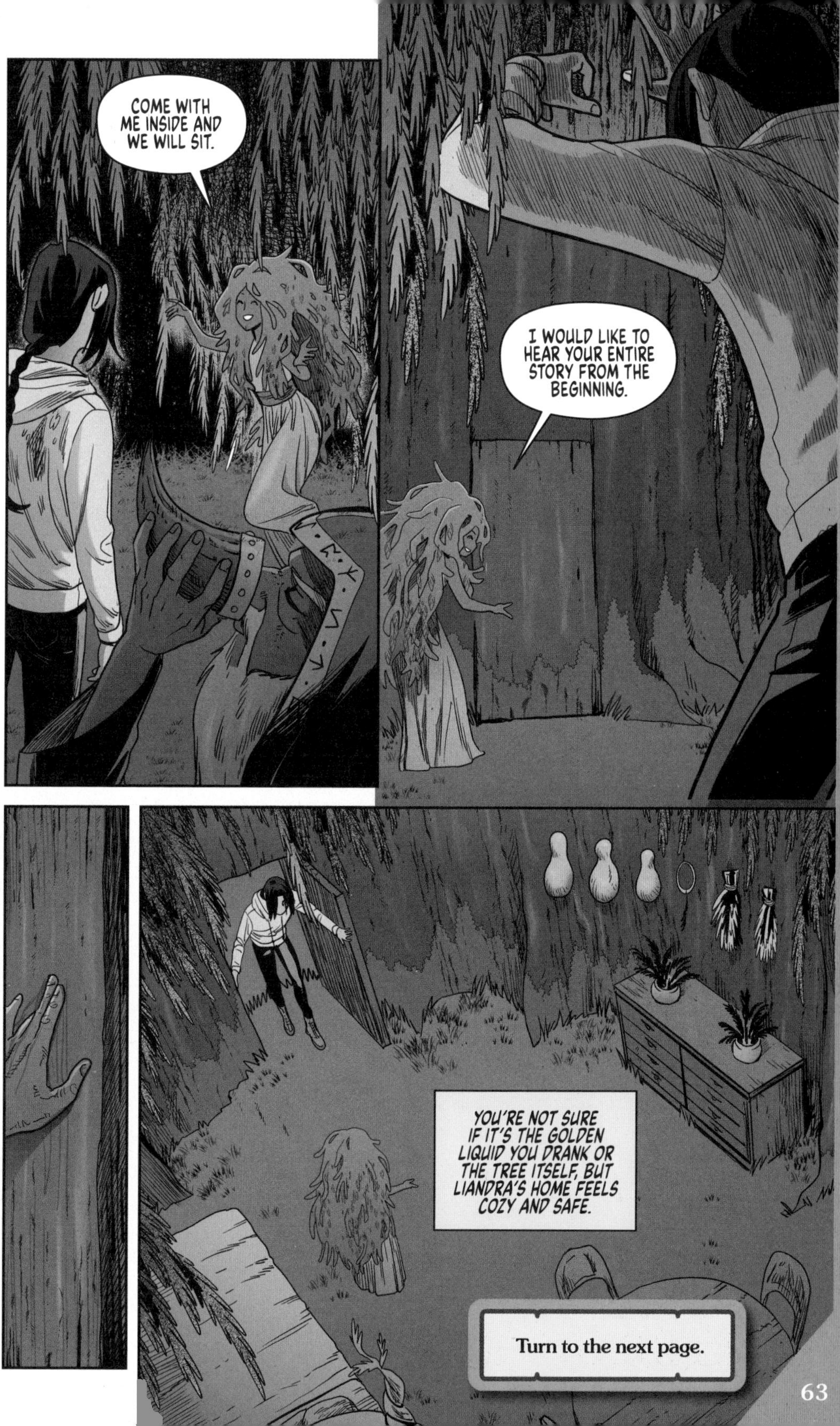
COME WITH ME INSIDE AND WE WILL SIT.
I WOULD LIKE TO HEAR YOUR ENTIRE STORY FROM THE BEGINNING.
YOU'RE NOT SURE IF IT'S THE GOLDEN LIQUID YOU DRANK OR THE TREE ITSELF, BUT LIANDRA'S HOME FEELS COZY AND SAFE.
Turn to the next page.

ALISTAIR GIVES LIANDRA AN OVERVIEW OF THE PAST FEW HOURS...

...OF THE DRUIDS, THE GOLDEN SICKLE, AND THE CHASE THROUGH THE FOREST THAT HAS BROUGHT YOU TO LIANDRA'S WILLOW.

YOU WERE MERELY MEANT TO BE A CONDUIT FOR THE TRANSFER OF THE SICKLE.

AND OF COURSE, SPREADING THE TRUTH ABOUT THE ANCIENT PROPHECY THAT THE DRUIDS HAVE DISCOVERED.

WHAT PROPHECY?

THE ORIGINAL BUILDERS OF THE HENGES WERE TRYING TO CREATE PERMANENT LINKS BETWEEN THE POWERS OF THE SUN AND THE MOON AND THE POWERS OF THE TREES AND OTHER PLANTS.

OH! I KNEW THERE WAS A REASON I DIDN'T KILL YOU WHEN I MET YOU, ALISTAIR!

HOW WOULD THEY DO THAT... CREATE THESE LINKS, I MEAN?

YOU IGNORE LIANDRA'S WEIRD COMMENT FOR NOW. YOU WANT TO KNOW MORE ABOUT THE POWER ALISTAIR HAS MENTIONED.

Go on to the next page.

LONG AGO, BEFORE THE DRUIDS EXISTED...

"...THERE WAS AN ANCIENT RACE OF PEOPLE WHO HAD TO MAKE SURE THAT THE LAND WAS GOING TO BE FRUITFUL AND NOT BARREN.

"YOU WILL FIND THAT THERE ARE MANY MYTHS AND STORIES ABOUT THE LAND FALLING INTO A PHASE WHERE CROPS WITHERED AND DIED.

"THESE STORIES ARE BASED IN FACT, AND WE ARE ABOUT TO ENTER ANOTHER SUCH PHASE.

"I BELIEVED THAT WE COULD STOP THE NEW BARREN PHASE FROM EVER OCCURRING.

"OTHER MEMBERS OF THE SUNS WANTED TO RECLAIM THE FERTILITY OF THE LAND AND BECOME THE JUST ARBITERS OF A NEW WORLD.

"THE GOLDEN SICKLE IS A KEY ELEMENT TO ENSURING THE CONTINUED FERTILITY OF THE LAND, BUT..."

Turn to the next page.

...THE SICKLE CAN ALSO ENSURE THAT IT WILL REMAIN A WASTELAND. IT ALL DEPENDS ON ITS USE.

LIANDRA, DO YOU HAVE ANY MORE OF THAT SAP-HEALTH DRINK?

I'M...I'M NOT FEELING VERY WELL ALL OF A SUDDEN.

LOOKS LIKE ＝KOFF＝ THEY MADE IT TO THE SACRED GROVE.

DRINK THIS.

WHATEVER IT IS THAT LIANDRA GIVES HIM, YOU CAN TELL ALISTAIR PERKS UP ALMOST IMMEDIATELY.

LISTEN TO ME...YOU MUST STOP THEM FROM FULFILLING THE PROPHECY OF THE BARREN LAND.

Go on to the next page.

THE GOLDEN SICKLE IS THE KEY TO THE RITUAL OF RENEWAL.

THEY NEED TO MAKE THE RITUAL SACRIFICE AT STONEHENGE BEFORE FOUR DAYS HAVE PASSED AFTER THE SOLSTICE.

IF THEY DON'T... ≋KOFF≋...THE LAND WILL CONTINUE AS IT...AS IT IS...

ALISTAIR!

ARGH!

QUICK! TAKE THIS KNIFE AND CUT SOME OF THE CATTAILS DOWN BY THE SWAMP.

THEN CUT A STRIP OF BARK FROM THE SIDE OF THIS TREE...

Turn to the next page.

...BRING BOTH TO ME AS FAST AS YOU CAN!

THE KNIFE IN YOUR HAND FEELS ROUGH.

VERY DIFFERENT THAN THE GOLDEN SICKLE'S SMOOTH SURFACE YOU'VE BEEN HOLDING THE LAST DAY.

HAS IT REALLY ONLY BEEN ONE DAY?

YOU CUT THROUGH THE CATTAILS, AND THEY FALL INTO YOUR HANDS LIKE SHEAVES OF WHEAT CUT BY THE SHARPEST SCYTHE.

IT THEN TAKES ONLY A MOMENT TO CUT A LONG STRIP OF WILLOW BARK FROM THE MASSIVE TREE.

IT'S AS IF YOU CAN FEEL THE WHOLE TREE SHUDDER AS YOU COLLECT IT.

Go on to the next page.

HURRY! BRING THEM TO ME!

I NEED THE KNIFE.

HE DOESN'T HAVE MUCH TIME...

...UNGH...

IF WE'RE LUCKY, THIS SHOULD KEEP HIM ALIVE A LITTLE LONGER...

...AT LEAST UNTIL YOU GET THERE.

Turn to the next page.

If you decide that the best chance to find and stop the druids is to go to Stonehenge, turn to page 76.

If you choose to go to the Sacred Grove, turn to page 84.

YOU AND ALISTAIR WALK UNTIL YOU REACH A SMALL TOWN WITH A PUB.

WE NEED TO TALK TO THE POLICE...

...CAN YOU HELP US? PLEASE?

ARE YOU OKAY? WHAT HAPPENED TO YOU TWO?

IT'S...IT'S A LONG STORY. CAN YOU PLEASE JUST TELL US WHERE TO FIND THE POLICE STATION?

WE DON'T HAVE A LOCAL STATION HERE, THE CLOSEST ONE IS TWO TOWNS AWAY, BUT I'LL CALL THEM FOR YOU.

THANK YOU... TELL THEM IT'S URGENT.

YOUR ONLY HOPE IS THAT WITH ALISTAIR CORROBORATING YOUR STORY, THE POLICE WILL TAKE YOU SERIOUSLY.

YOU KNOW HOW UNREAL THE EVENTS OF THE LAST FEW HOURS WILL SOUND...

Turn to the next page.

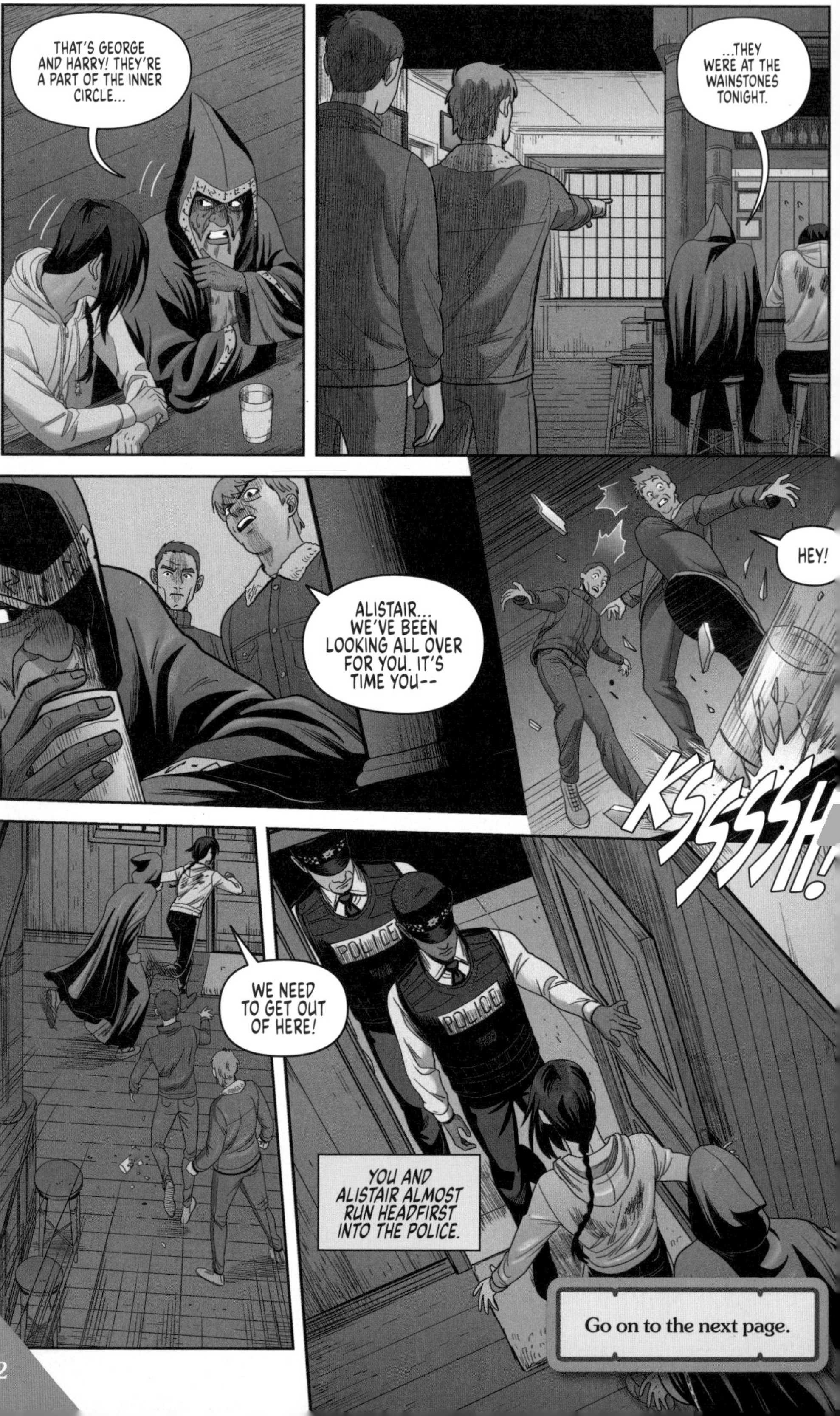
THAT'S GEORGE AND HARRY! THEY'RE A PART OF THE INNER CIRCLE...
...THEY WERE AT THE WAINSTONES TONIGHT.
ALISTAIR... WE'VE BEEN LOOKING ALL OVER FOR YOU. IT'S TIME YOU--
HEY!
KSSSSH!
WE NEED TO GET OUT OF HERE!
YOU AND ALISTAIR ALMOST RUN HEADFIRST INTO THE POLICE.
Go on to the next page.

THAT'S THEM, OFFICERS...THE ONES I CALLED ABOUT.

I HAVE A BAD FEELING ABOUT THIS...

YOU THINK ALISTAIR IS JUST BEING DRAMATIC. THE POLICE ARRIVING JUST AS THE DRUIDS FIND YOU SEEMS LIKE PERFECT TIMING...

...UNTIL YOU REALIZE THAT ALISTAIR'S SUSPICIONS WEREN'T UNWARRANTED.

LET'S GET YOU DOWN TO THE STATION TO ANSWER A FEW QUESTIONS, OKAY?

HEY! WHAT ARE YOU DOING?

THOSE ARE THE MEN YOU WANT!

I'M SORRY... BUT WE'VE NEVER SEEN THESE PEOPLE BEFORE.

WE JUST STOPPED IN FOR A DRINK, AND THEY STARTED THROWING THINGS.

THEY'RE LYING! THEY KIDNAPPED ME!

I THINK WE'VE GOT THE REAL KIDNAPPER RIGHT HERE.

THE OFFICERS TAKE YOU AND ALISTAIR BACK TO THE STATION FOR QUESTIONING...

Turn to the next page.

73

...WHERE THEY PUT YOU IN SEPARATE INTERROGATION ROOMS AND ASK YOU TO REPEAT YOUR STORY A NUMBER OF TIMES.

BUT NO MATTER HOW MANY TIMES YOU EXPLAIN THE EVENTS OF THE LAST DAY, THEY DON'T BELIEVE YOU.

YOU ONLY THINK THESE THINGS ARE TRUE BECAUSE OF WHAT ALISTAIR SHEPHERD HAS DONE TO YOU.

WE ALSO KNOW THAT YOU FLED FROM THE BRITISH MUSEUM WITH A STOLEN ARTIFACT, PRESUMABLY INTENDED TO GIVE TO ALISTAIR.

HE HAS CLEARLY BRAINWASHED YOU IN SOME WAY.

BUT WE CALLED YOU!

WE WERE ALREADY ON OUR WAY.

WE GOT THE CALL FROM HQ TO LOOK FOR YOU IN GREAT BROUGHTON HOURS BEFORE YOU WERE SPOTTED IN THE PUB.

WE KNOW THAT THIS IS WHAT YOU THINK HAPPENED...

Go on to the next page.

"...BUT WE ARE GOING TO GET YOU THE HELP YOU NEED."

THE POLICE HAVE YOU ADMITTED TO THE PSYCHIATRIC WARD OF A NEARBY HOSPITAL.

AFTER A DAY AND A HALF, TWIG MANAGES TO GET YOU RELEASED, AND YOU LEARN THAT ALISTAIR HAS ALLEGEDLY "ESCAPED" POLICE CUSTODY.

YOU NEVER SEE HIM OR HEAR OF THE GOLDEN SICKLE AGAIN.

THE END

MONTHS LATER, YOU THINK OF HIM WHEN A DROUGHT KILLS THE ENTIRE GERMAN WHEAT HARVEST...

DO YOUR BEST TO KEEP HIM ALIVE, LIANDRA.

I'M GOING TO STONEHENGE TO TRY TO PREVENT THEM FROM PERFORMING THE RITUAL ALISTAIR MENTIONED.

THE DRUIDS HAVE MANY DIFFERENT RITUALS...MANY WAYS OF APPEALING TO THE POWERS OF THE GREEN. BUT THE ONE ALISTAIR WAS TALKING ABOUT...

...I THINK HE WAS TALKING ABOUT HUMAN SACRIFICE.

HERE... TAKE THIS WITH YOU...

IT WILL PROVIDE POWER TO YOU IF YOU DO FIND THE DRUIDS.

WHAT THEY ARE PLANNING TO DO TO THE EARTH IS WRONG...YOU MUST STOP THEM.

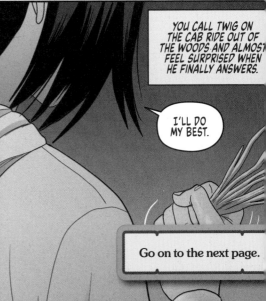

YOU CALL TWIG ON THE CAB RIDE OUT OF THE WOODS AND ALMOST FEEL SURPRISED WHEN HE FINALLY ANSWERS.

I'LL DO MY BEST.

Go on to the next page.

76

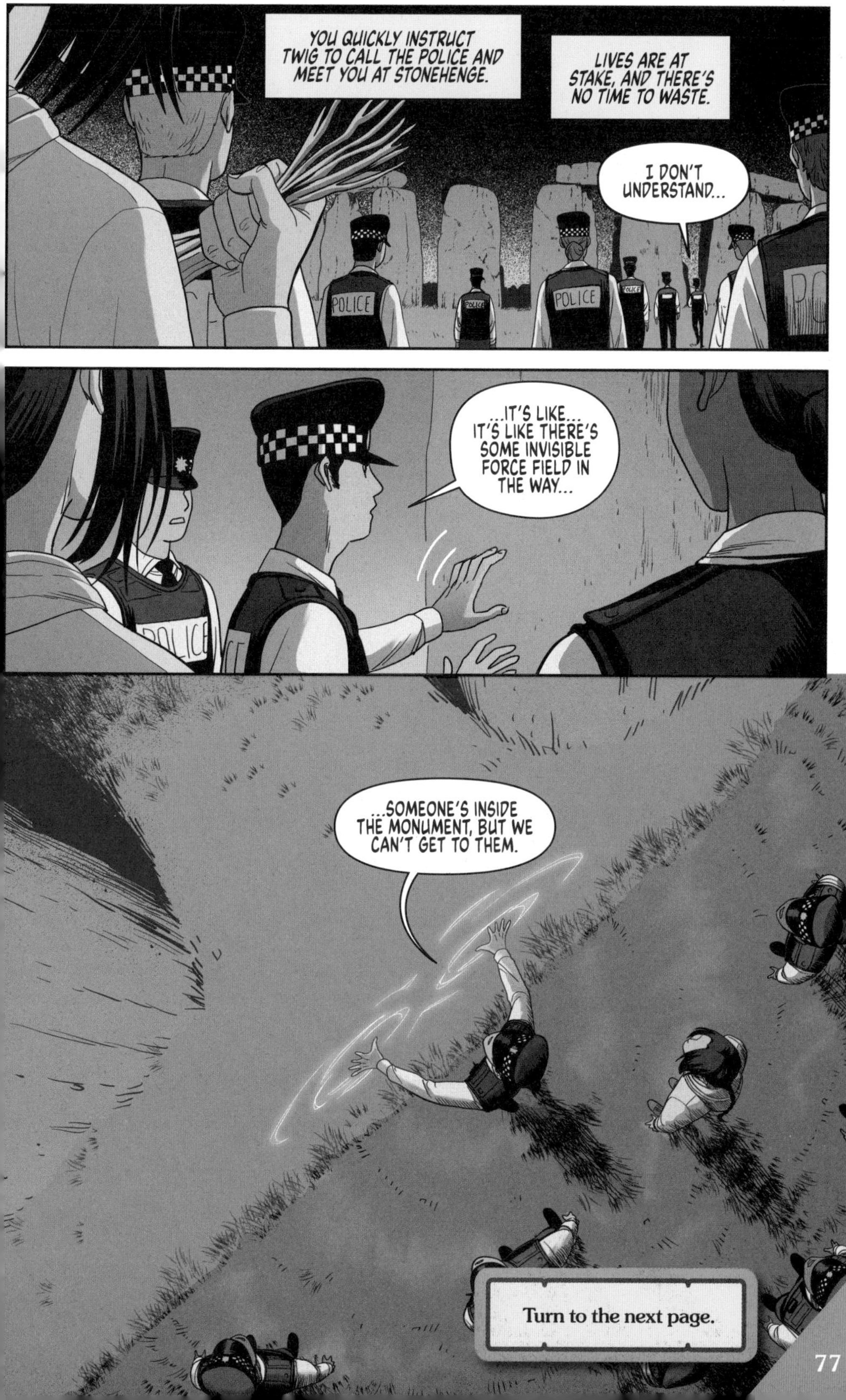
YOU QUICKLY INSTRUCT TWIG TO CALL THE POLICE AND MEET YOU AT STONEHENGE.
LIVES ARE AT STAKE, AND THERE'S NO TIME TO WASTE.
I DON'T UNDERSTAND...
POLICE
POLICE
...IT'S LIKE... IT'S LIKE THERE'S SOME INVISIBLE FORCE FIELD IN THE WAY...
...SOMEONE'S INSIDE THE MONUMENT, BUT WE CAN'T GET TO THEM.

Turn to the next page.

AFTER THE TWELVE HOURS IT TOOK YOU TO REACH STONEHENGE FROM LIANDRA'S, AND WITH LIVES ON THE LINE...

I'VE NEVER SEEN ANYTHING LIKE IT IN MY ENTIRE LIFE.

...YOU CAN'T FAIL NOW.

AS YOU TAKE A STEP TOWARD THE BARRIER, YOU FEEL A TWITCHING SENSATION IN YOUR HAND.

IS THE WILLOW SWITCH TELLING YOU SOMETHING...?

Go on to the next page.

WHAT ARE YOU DOING?

I HAVE AN IDEA...

IS... IS THIS A *GOOD* THING?

I THINK IT IS.

THE BARRIER IS WARM AS YOU PASS THROUGH IT, WITH A CONSISTENCY ALMOST LIKE MOSS, THAT GIVES WAY AS YOU CROSS INTO THE MONUMENT.

FOLLOW ME.

Turn to the next page.

AS YOU ENTER THE MONUMENT, YOU BEGIN TO HEAR A DEEP CHANTING THAT FEELS LIKE IT'S VIBRATING AROUND THE STONES.

LOOK! THOSE MUST BE THEIR HUMAN SACRIFICES...

THE SCENE IS BLEAK AND FRIGHTENING, BUT YOU CAN'T LET THE TERROR BECOME PARALYZING.

Go on to the next page.

STOP!

WITHOUT THINKING, YOU RUSH FORWARD, INTO THE MIDDLE OF THE RITUAL.

YOU IMMEDIATELY GO TOWARD THE LEADER, HOPING THAT RETRIEVING THE SICKLE WILL INTERRUPT WHATEVER THEY'VE ALREADY STARTED.

WSSSSSH!

BUT AS THE WILLOW SWITCH AND THE SICKLE MEET...

...A FLASH OF LIGHT EXPLODES FROM THE IMPACT.

Turn to the next page.

81

BY THE TIME YOU GET BACK TO YOUR FEET, THE BARRIER IS DOWN AND THE POLICE ARE ARRESTING THE DRUIDS.

THE DRUIDS TRY TO ESCAPE, BUT THEY ARE ALL CAPTURED RATHER QUICKLY.

YOU STUMBLE TOWARD THE GOLDEN SICKLE, BUT YOU FEEL HEAVY, LIKE SOMETHING IS WEIGHING YOU DOWN.

YOUR VISION STARTS TO CLOUD...

...AND THE LAST THING YOU REMEMBER IS FALLING GENTLY INTO THE SOFT, GREEN GRASS.

Go on to the next page.

YOU WAKE UP IN A HOSPITAL ROOM BACK IN LONDON.

YOU'RE UP!

TWIG IS IN A WHEELCHAIR BY THE WINDOW AND EXPLAINS THAT HIS INJURIES KEPT HIM FROM MEETING YOU AT STONEHENGE.

THE POLICE WILL WANT TO TALK WITH YOU, BUT THE NURSE BROUGHT THAT IN A LITTLE BIT AGO.

IT'S A LETTER...

THE POLICE ARRESTED ALL OF THE DRUIDS AT THE MONUMENT, AND IT SEEMS YOU MANAGED TO DISRUPT THE RITUAL JUST IN TIME.

BUT THANKS TO AN ODD LETTER WRITTEN ON BIRCH BARK AND SMELLING OF BERRY JUICE...

...YOU LEARN THAT YOUR TRIP TO STONEHENGE WASN'T ENTIRELY SUCCESSFUL.

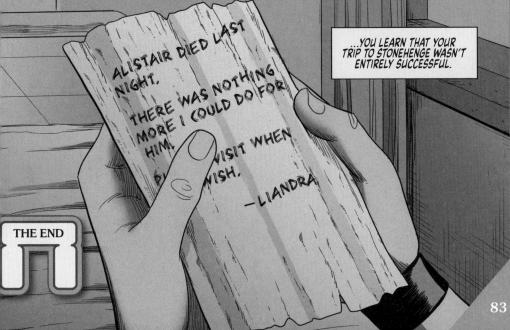

ALISTAIR DIED LAST NIGHT.

THERE WAS NOTHING MORE I COULD DO FOR HIM.

VISIT WHEN WISH.

—LIANDRA

THE END

83

YOU DECIDE TO VISIT THE SACRED GROVE, AND LIANDRA PROVIDES YOU WITH A MAP.

HER INSTRUCTIONS ARE VAGUE AND RELY HEAVILY ON NATURAL FEATURES THAT YOU DON'T KNOW, BUT YOU EVENTUALLY FIGURE OUT THAT SHE IS REFERRING TO THE ROYAL FOREST OF DEAN IN GLOUCESTER.

YOU ARRIVE JUST AS THE SUN IS SETTING AND WANDER THROUGH THE TALL TREES, LOOKING AT THE SCULPTURES THAT LINE THE MAIN TRAIL.

A FEW METAL DEER POKE OUT FROM THE BRUSH, AND YOU CAN'T HELP BUT NOTICE THAT THEY HAVE A SLIGHTLY SINISTER APPEARANCE.

NOW WHERE IS THE SACRED GROVE?

JUST AHEAD...

Go on to the next page.

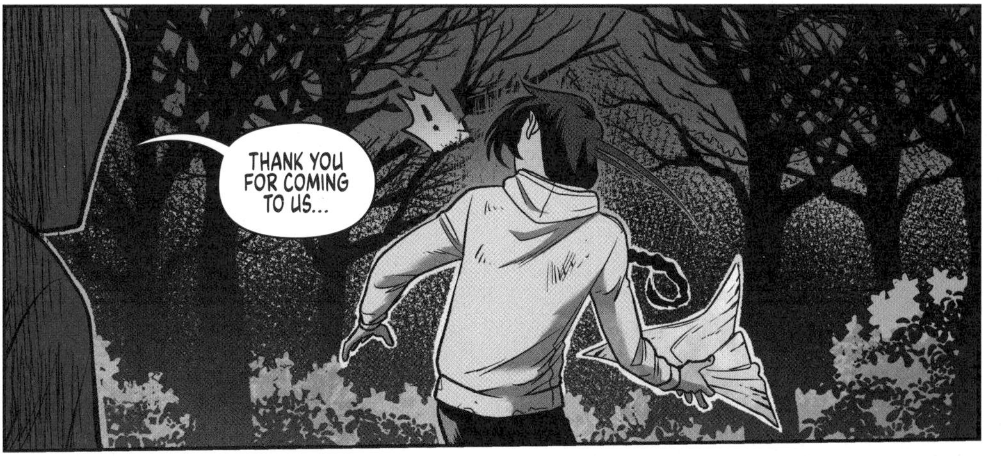
THANK YOU FOR COMING TO US...

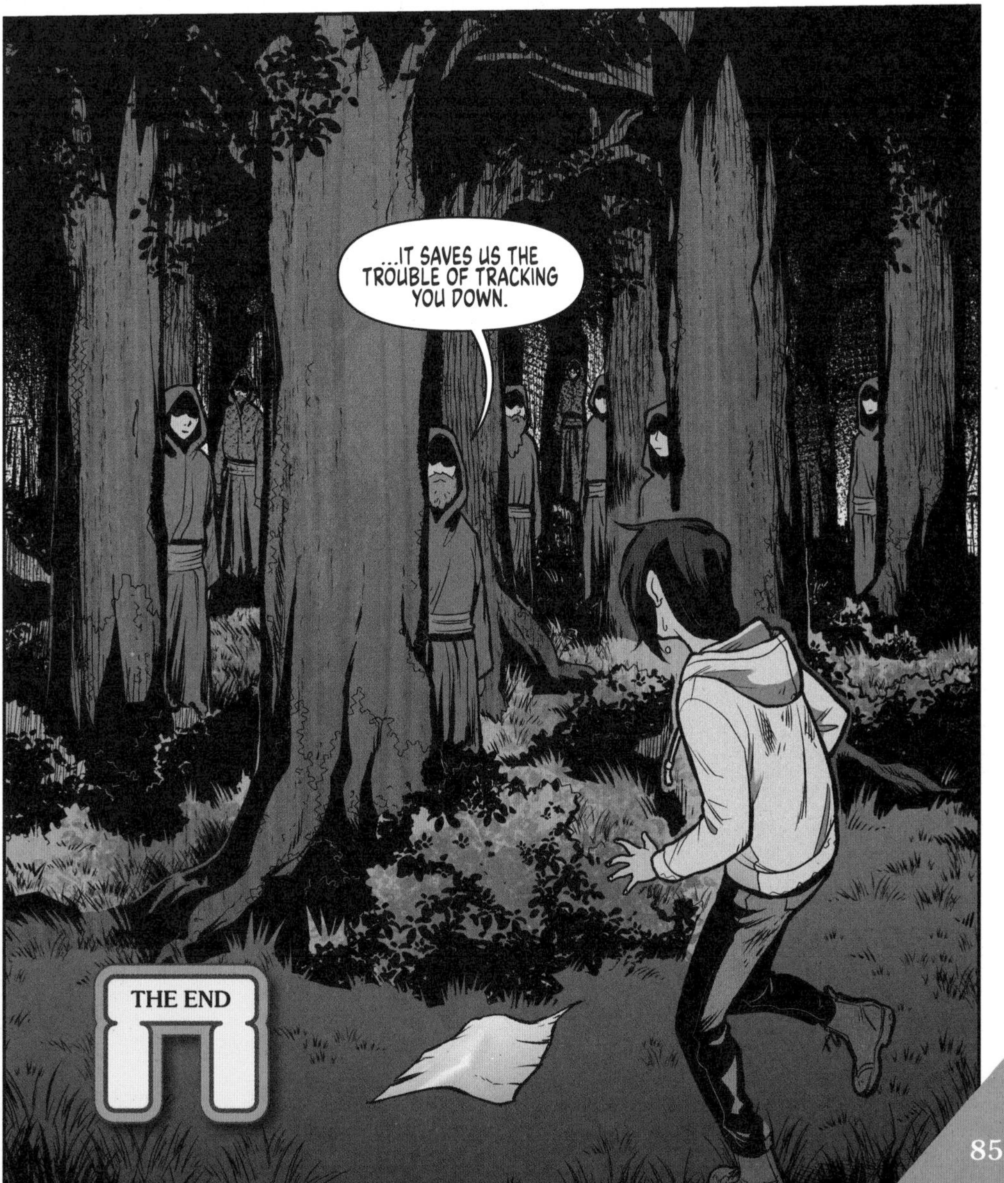
...IT SAVES US THE TROUBLE OF TRACKING YOU DOWN.
THE END

YOU CAN TAKE ME TO ALISTAIR?

OF COURSE. HE AND THE OTHER ARCH-DRUIDS OFTEN USE OUR ENTRANCE...

...COME WITH ME.

WELCOME, HUMAN!

QUIET, DANI. WE NEED TO GET BY THE POLICE PERIMETER.

YOU THINK YOU CAN DISTRACT THE GUARDS FOR A MOMENT?

YOU GOT IT, BOSS.

ONE DISTRACTION, COMING RIGHT UP!

THESE PEOPLE ARE PRETTY GOOD AT ROLE-PLAYING, YOU THINK TO YOURSELF WHILE WATCHING DANI BOUND AWAY CHEERFULLY.

Go on to the next page.

YOU WONDER HOW IT'S POSSIBLE THAT **THIS** GROUP HAS A SECRET ENTRANCE TO STONEHENGE...

...BUT BEFORE YOU CAN RETHINK YOUR DECISION, ELAINE BEGINS QUICKLY PULLING YOU AWAY FROM THE CROWD OF PEOPLE AT THE MONUMENT'S ENTRANCE.

NOW'S OUR CHANCE!

IT'S JUST BEHIND THIS BARROW.

WHAT IS? WHAT EXACTLY ARE WE...?

Turn to the next page.

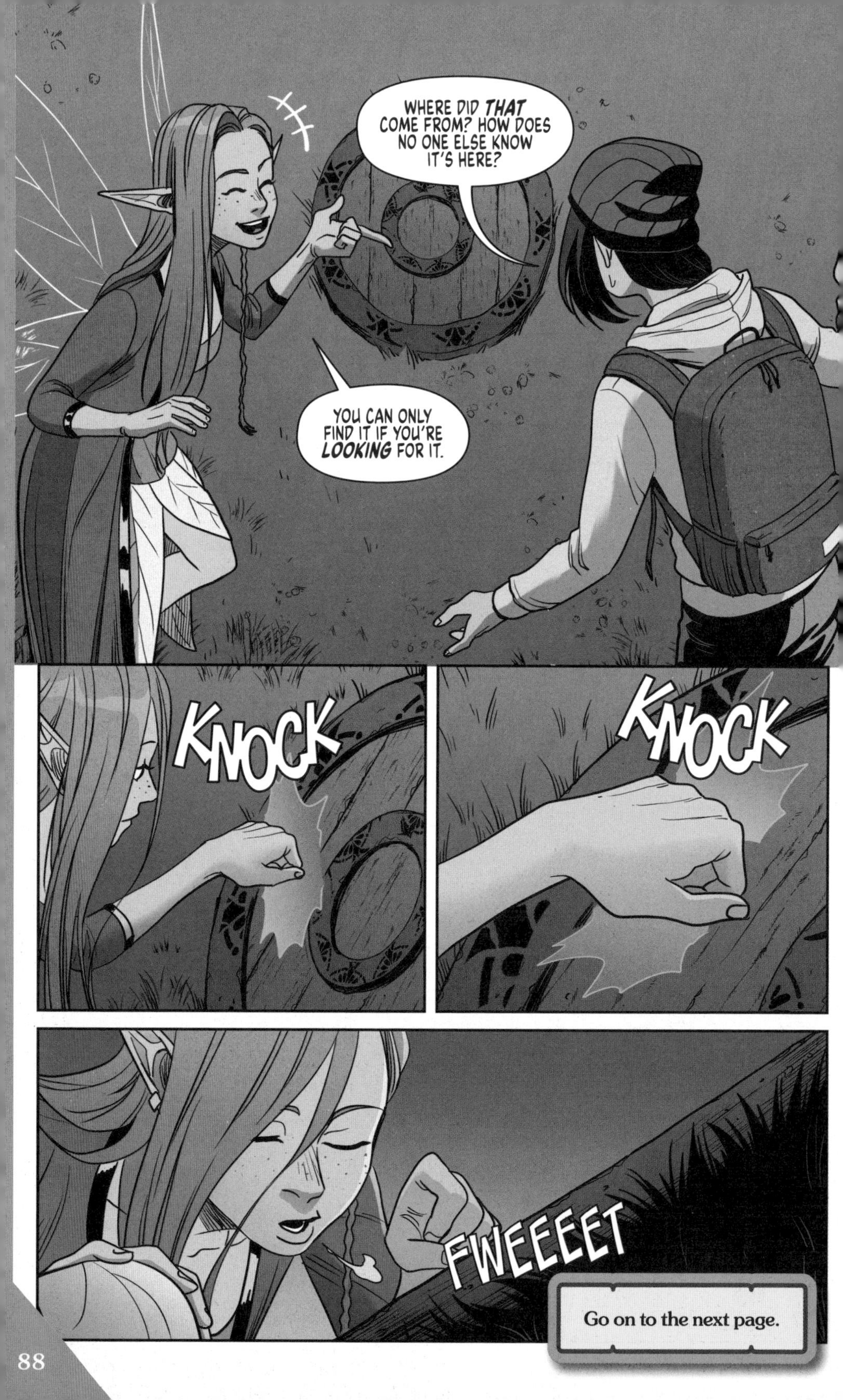
WHERE DID THAT COME FROM? HOW DOES NO ONE ELSE KNOW IT'S HERE?
YOU CAN ONLY FIND IT IF YOU'RE LOOKING FOR IT.
KNOCK
KNOCK
FWEEEET
Go on to the next page.

AS THE DOOR SWINGS INWARD, YOU CAN SEE NOTHING OF THE PATH BEFORE YOU.

THE DARKNESS FEELS... UNINVITING, TO SAY THE LEAST.

BUT YOU THINK OF TWIG AND ALISTAIR. THIS MIGHT JUST BE THE ONLY WAY INTO STONEHENGE.

SLAM

ELAINE?

YOU CAN FEEL YOUR HEART RACING...POUNDING IN YOUR CHEST.

WAS THIS A MISTAKE?

Turn to the next page.

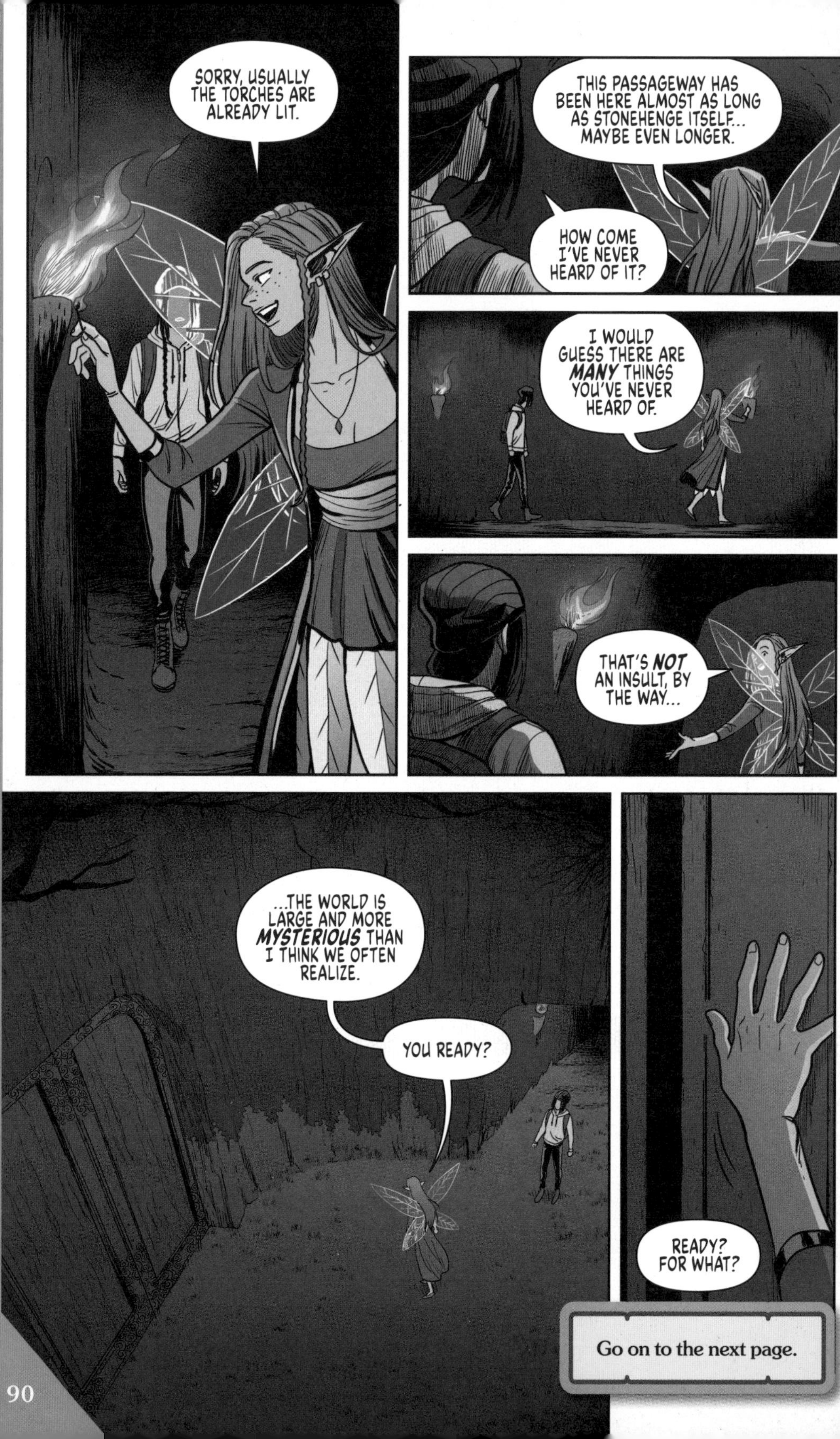
SORRY, USUALLY THE TORCHES ARE ALREADY LIT.
THIS PASSAGEWAY HAS BEEN HERE ALMOST AS LONG AS STONEHENGE ITSELF... MAYBE EVEN LONGER.
HOW COME I'VE NEVER HEARD OF IT?
I WOULD GUESS THERE ARE *MANY* THINGS YOU'VE NEVER HEARD OF.
THAT'S *NOT* AN INSULT, BY THE WAY...
...THE WORLD IS LARGE AND MORE *MYSTERIOUS* THAN I THINK WE OFTEN REALIZE.
YOU READY?
READY? FOR WHAT?

Go on to the next page.

FOR *THIS.*

YOU FIND YOURSELF IN ONE OF THE
LARGEST ROOMS YOU'VE EVER SEEN.
THE TABLES ARE ALL FILLED WITH FOOD
AND MORE PEOPLE DRESSED AS FAIRIES.

IT'S AN INCREDIBLE SCENE,
BUT YOU DON'T SEE A SINGLE
PERSON DRESSED AS A DRUID.

Turn to the next page.

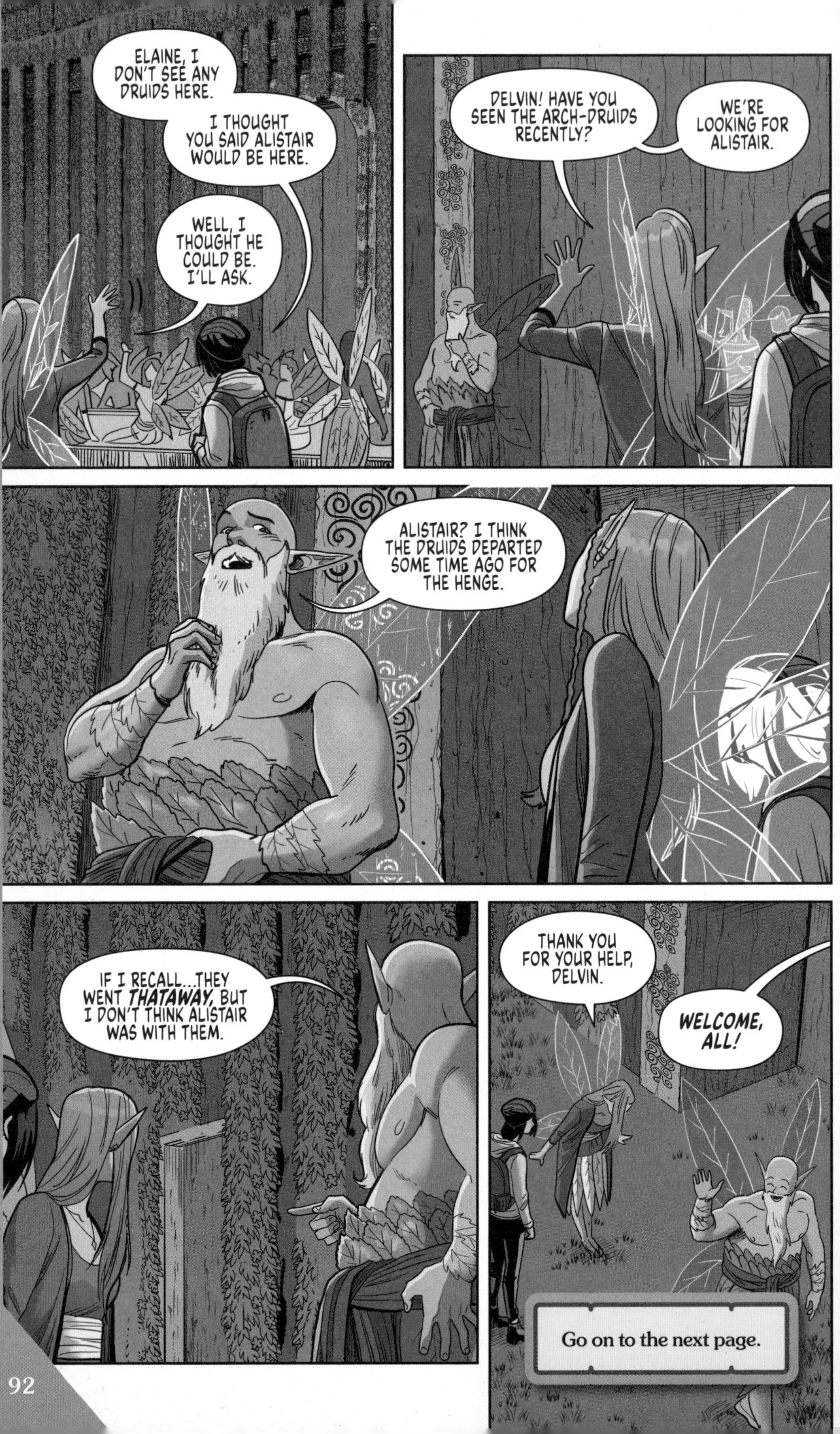
ELAINE, I DON'T SEE ANY DRUIDS HERE.
I THOUGHT YOU SAID ALISTAIR WOULD BE HERE.
WELL, I THOUGHT HE COULD BE. I'LL ASK.
DELVIN! HAVE YOU SEEN THE ARCH-DRUIDS RECENTLY?
WE'RE LOOKING FOR ALISTAIR.
ALISTAIR? I THINK THE DRUIDS DEPARTED SOME TIME AGO FOR THE HENGE.
IF I RECALL...THEY WENT *THATAWAY,* BUT I DON'T THINK ALISTAIR WAS WITH THEM.
THANK YOU FOR YOUR HELP, DELVIN.
WELCOME, ALL!
Go on to the next page.

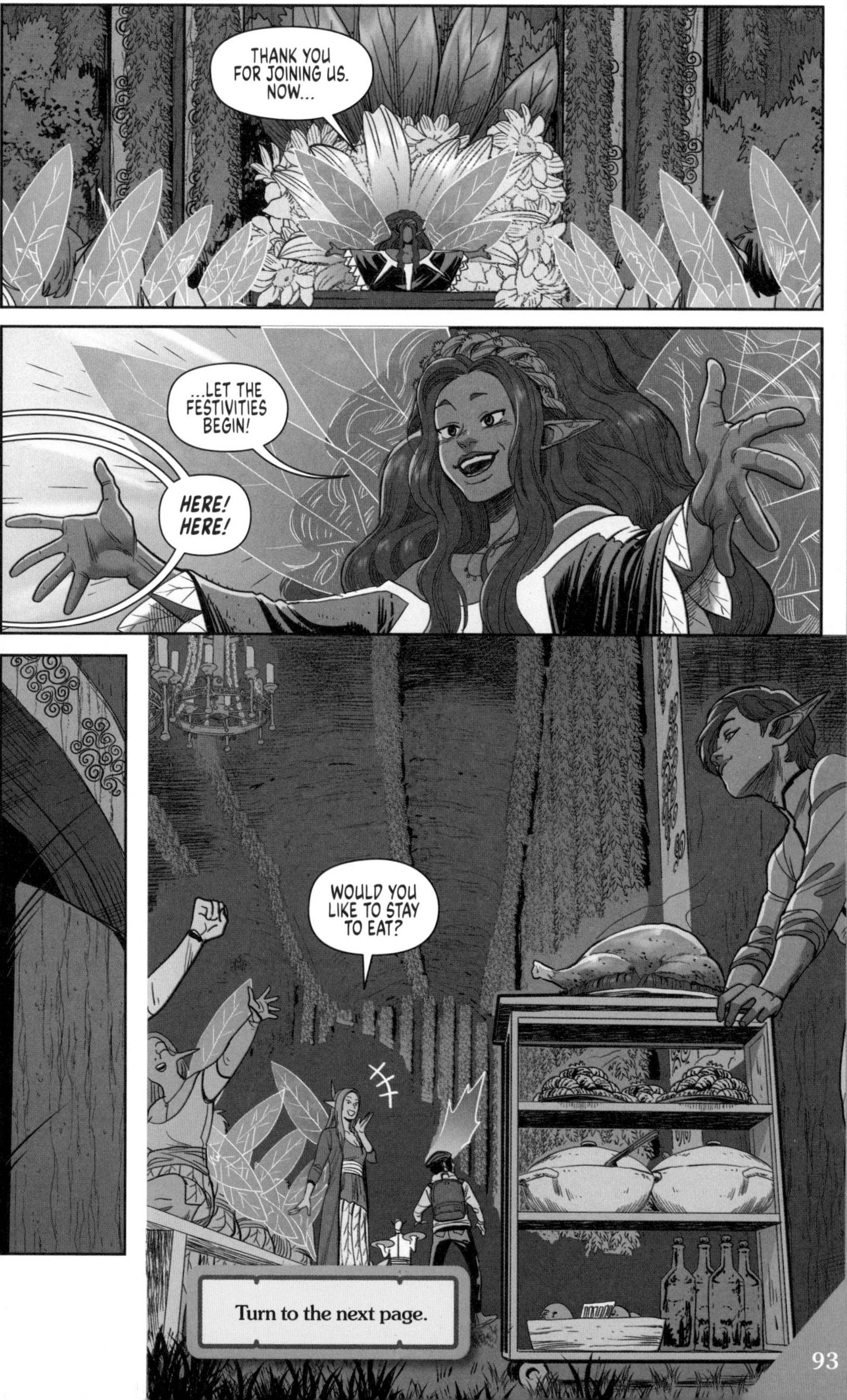
THANK YOU FOR JOINING US. NOW...
...LET THE FESTIVITIES BEGIN!
HERE! HERE!
WOULD YOU LIKE TO STAY TO EAT?

Turn to the next page.

THE FOOD LOOKS AND SMELLS AMAZING...

...AND YOU SUDDENLY REALIZE HOW HUNGRY YOU ARE.

BUT YOU CAME HERE TO FIND ALISTAIR, NOT HAVE A FEAST.

I'D LIKE TO FIND ALISTAIR.

IT WOULD BE HARD TO FIND ALISTAIR ON AN EMPTY STOMACH.

Go on to the next page.

94

SURELY IT COULDN'T HURT TO HAVE *ONE* BITE?

ALL YOU WANT IS TO POP THE DELICIOUS-LOOKING CAKE IN YOUR MOUTH... BUT SUDDENLY AN OLD SAYING COMES TO MIND...

"EAT A FAIRY'S FOOD, BECOME A FAIRY'S SLAVE."

THAT'S JUST A SAYING, RIGHT?

CAN I INTEREST EITHER OF YOU IN SOMETHING SWEET?

MAYBE IT'S TIME YOU RETURN TO THE CAR PARK TO SEE IF ALISTAIR IS WAITING ON YOU AFTER ALL...

If you decide to stay with Elaine in the large hall and risk eating the fairy feast before continuing your search for Alistair, turn to the next page.

If you choose to return above ground to look for Alistair immediately, turn to page 131.

IT COULDN'T HURT JUST TO EAT A LITTLE BIT OF FAIRY FOOD.

I ADMIT I'M *STARVED*.

WE PREFER TO BE CALLED *FAE* THESE DAYS. FAIRY IS A LITTLE OLD SCHOOL.

RIGHT, *FAE* FOOD, THEN.

EAT UP!

YOU'VE NEVER SEEN A FEAST QUITE LIKE THIS. FROM THE FAE GATHERED AROUND THE TABLES OF THE LARGE HALL...

...TO THE MOST DELICIOUS FOOD YOU'VE EVER EATEN.

Go on to the next page.

YOU BEGIN TO PUT ALISTAIR EVEN FURTHER FROM YOUR MIND AS MORE PIES AND ICE CREAM ARRIVE AT THE TABLE.

I DON'T CARE IF I DO BECOME YOUR SLAVE...

...THIS IS THE *BEST* MEAL I'VE EVER EATEN.

RIIING
RIIING

IT'S THE QUEEN...SHE'S ABOUT TO SPEAK.

Turn to the next page.

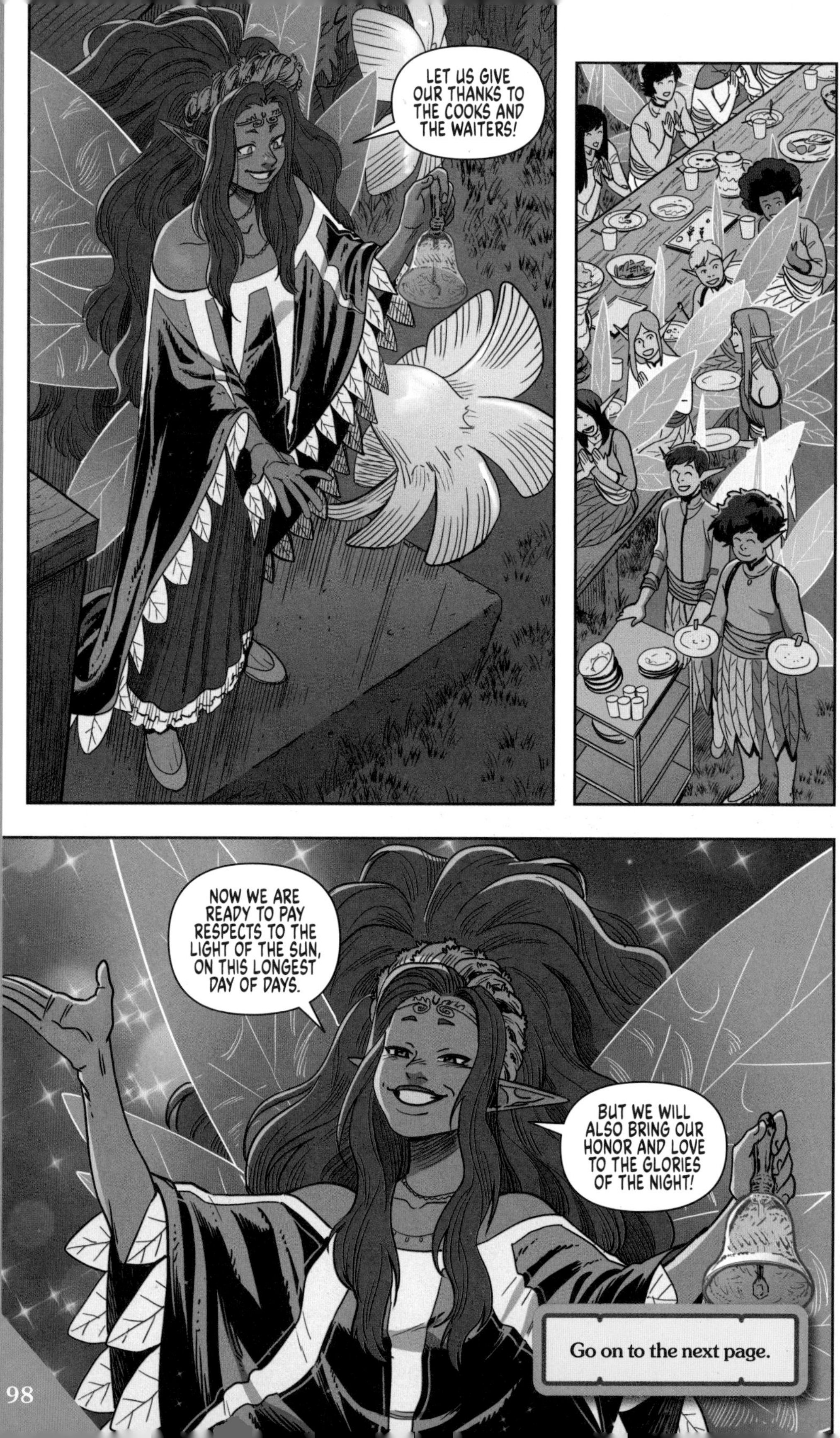
LET US GIVE OUR THANKS TO THE COOKS AND THE WAITERS!
NOW WE ARE READY TO PAY RESPECTS TO THE LIGHT OF THE SUN, ON THIS LONGEST DAY OF DAYS.
BUT WE WILL ALSO BRING OUR HONOR AND LOVE TO THE GLORIES OF THE NIGHT!

Go on to the next page.

THE DOORS OPEN FOR THE QUEEN AS IF BY MAGIC, AND THE OTHERS IN THE HALL BEGIN TO FALL IN LINE BEHIND HER.

COME.

THE FAE BEGIN SINGING, THEIR WORDS ECHOING AROUND THE WALLS OF THE NARROW TUNNEL.

SUN DOWN, SUN DOWN, MOON RISE, MOON RISE...

...WHEN IT DROPS...

IF YOU HAVE YOUR DIRECTIONS STRAIGHT, THIS TUNNEL SHOULD LEAD RIGHT TOWARD STONEHENGE.

...WISE EYES, WISE EYES!

Turn to the next page.

AS YOU EXIT THE TUNNEL, YOU SEE THE LAST GLOW OF SUN FROM THE LONGEST DAY OF THE YEAR.

BUT ALL THAT YOU CAN SEE IS UNTOUCHED GREEN.

AS IF NO ONE WAS EVER HERE AT ALL.

LET US KNEEL!

AS YOU EXIT THE TUNNEL INTO THE CENTER OF THE MONUMENT, YOU LOOK AROUND FOR ANY TRACE OF POLICE OR THE DOZENS OF PEOPLE WHO WERE IN THE PARKING LOT.

Go on to the next page.

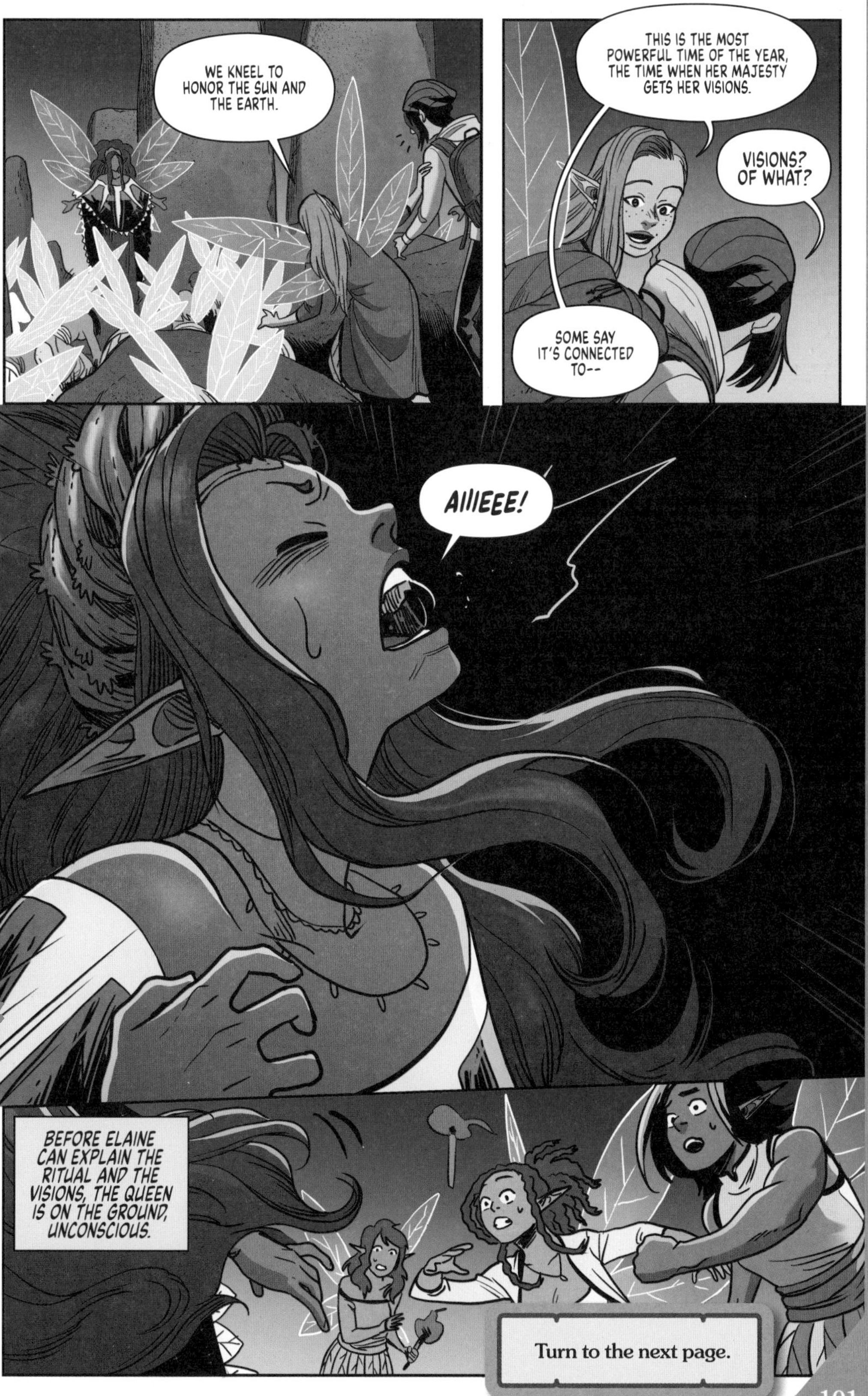

WE KNEEL TO HONOR THE SUN AND THE EARTH.
THIS IS THE MOST POWERFUL TIME OF THE YEAR, THE TIME WHEN HER MAJESTY GETS HER VISIONS.
VISIONS? OF WHAT?
SOME SAY IT'S CONNECTED TO--
AIIIEEE!
BEFORE ELAINE CAN EXPLAIN THE RITUAL AND THE VISIONS, THE QUEEN IS ON THE GROUND, UNCONSCIOUS.

Turn to the next page.

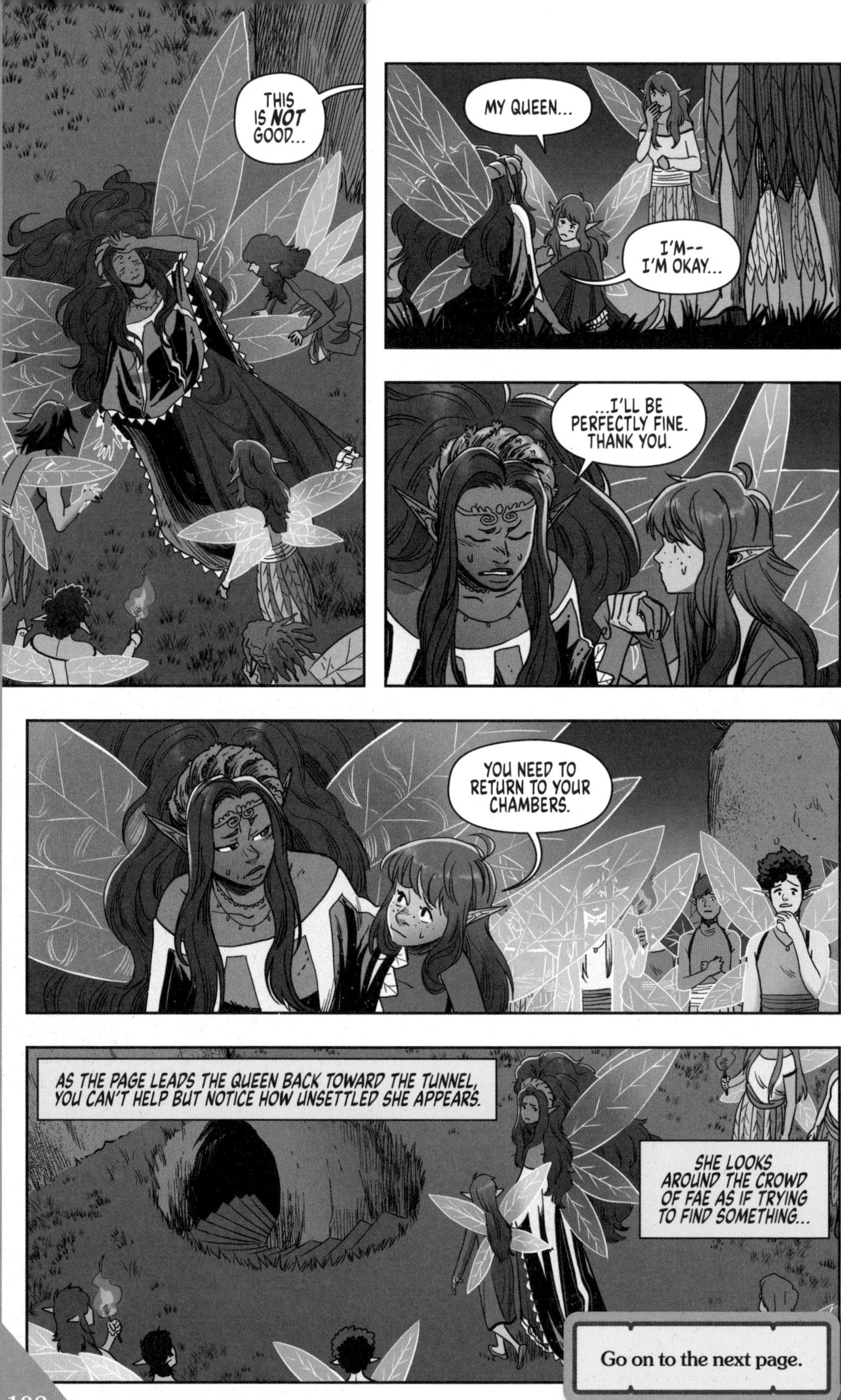
THIS IS NOT GOOD...
MY QUEEN...
I'M-- I'M OKAY...
...I'LL BE PERFECTLY FINE. THANK YOU.
YOU NEED TO RETURN TO YOUR CHAMBERS.
AS THE PAGE LEADS THE QUEEN BACK TOWARD THE TUNNEL, YOU CAN'T HELP BUT NOTICE HOW UNSETTLED SHE APPEARS.
SHE LOOKS AROUND THE CROWD OF FAE AS IF TRYING TO FIND SOMETHING...

Go on to the next page.

...OR SOMEONE.

THE QUEEN LOCKS EYES WITH YOU AND POINTS.

YOU CAN FEEL THE EYES OF ALL THE OTHER FAE ON YOU, AS IF BURNING THROUGH YOUR SKIN.

WHY YOU?

I'VE NEVER SEEN ANYTHING LIKE THIS... ...AND I'VE BEEN ATTENDING FOR 332 YEARS!

THE QUEEN WOULD LIKE TO SEE YOU IN HER AUDIENCE CHAMBER. PLEASE FOLLOW ME, IF YOU WOULD BE SO KIND.

YOU DON'T OFFER A VERBAL AGREEMENT, BUT SIMPLY FOLLOW THE PAGE BACK TOWARD THE TUNNEL.

"THE SOLSTICE IS MORE THAN JUST A TRADITION..."

Turn to the next page.

...AT THE SETTING OF THE SOLSTICE SUN ON MIDSUMMER'S EVE...

...KNOWLEDGE OF THE *FUTURE* IS GIVEN TO THE ONE WHO KNOWS HOW TO ASK.

THE HENGE ALSO ACTS AS AN *ENERGY VORTEX*. IT BALANCES THE FORCES OF EARTH-- BRINGING IN GRATITUDE, CLEANSING THE GREED AND HATE.

AND THE BALANCING OCCURS FOR JUST A FEW MINUTES EACH SOLSTICE. BUT IT IS ESSENTIAL TO OUR--AND YOUR--SURVIVAL.

WHAT HAPPENED TONIGHT?

I SAW... I SAW SOMETHING *TERRIBLE*.

A DARK FATE THAT IS GOING TO BEFALL THE FAE *AND* THE HUMANS.

Go on to the next page.

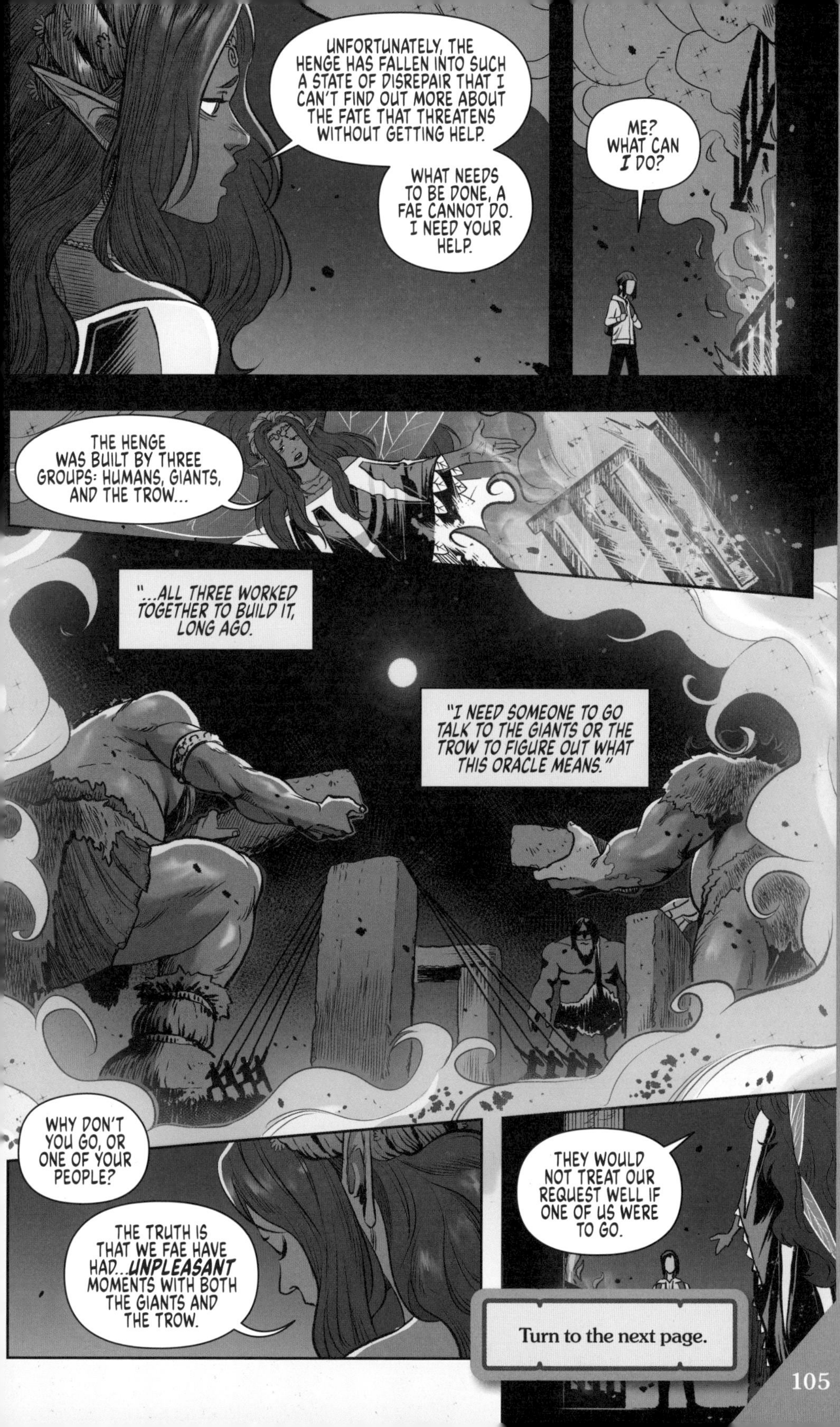
UNFORTUNATELY, THE HENGE HAS FALLEN INTO SUCH A STATE OF DISREPAIR THAT I CAN'T FIND OUT MORE ABOUT THE FATE THAT THREATENS WITHOUT GETTING HELP.
WHAT NEEDS TO BE DONE, A FAE CANNOT DO. I NEED YOUR HELP.
ME? WHAT CAN *I* DO?
THE HENGE WAS BUILT BY THREE GROUPS: HUMANS, GIANTS, AND THE TROW...
"...ALL THREE WORKED TOGETHER TO BUILD IT, LONG AGO.
"I NEED SOMEONE TO GO TALK TO THE GIANTS OR THE TROW TO FIGURE OUT WHAT THIS ORACLE MEANS."
WHY DON'T YOU GO, OR ONE OF YOUR PEOPLE?
THE TRUTH IS THAT WE FAE HAVE HAD...**UNPLEASANT** MOMENTS WITH BOTH THE GIANTS AND THE TROW.
THEY WOULD NOT TREAT OUR REQUEST WELL IF ONE OF US WERE TO GO.

Turn to the next page.

If you choose to visit the giants, go on to the next page.

If you choose to go to the trow, turn to page 126.

AFTER CHOOSING TO VISIT THE GIANTS, YOU SPENT THE NIGHT AS A GUEST OF THE QUEEN.

YOU WERE PROVIDED WITH A LAVISH ROOM AND THE MOST COMFORTABLE BED YOU'VE EVER SLEPT IN.

ELAINE ACCOMPANIES YOU THE NEXT MORNING AS YOUR GUIDE, LEAVING THE HENGE THROUGH YET **ANOTHER** SECRET EXIT.

YOU SPEND THE DAY HIKING TOGETHER THROUGH A LONG VALLEY, NEVER SEEMING TO TIRE DESPITE THE LARGE DISTANCE YOU'VE TRAVELED ON FOOT.

WE'RE ALMOST THERE...

YOU'RE NOT ENTIRELY SURE WHERE **THERE** IS. THE MOUNTAINS AHEAD OF YOU LOOK BIGGER THAN ANYTHING YOU'VE EVER SEEN IN ENGLAND.

THE QUESTION IS: ARE YOU STILL **IN** ENGLAND?

Turn to the next page.

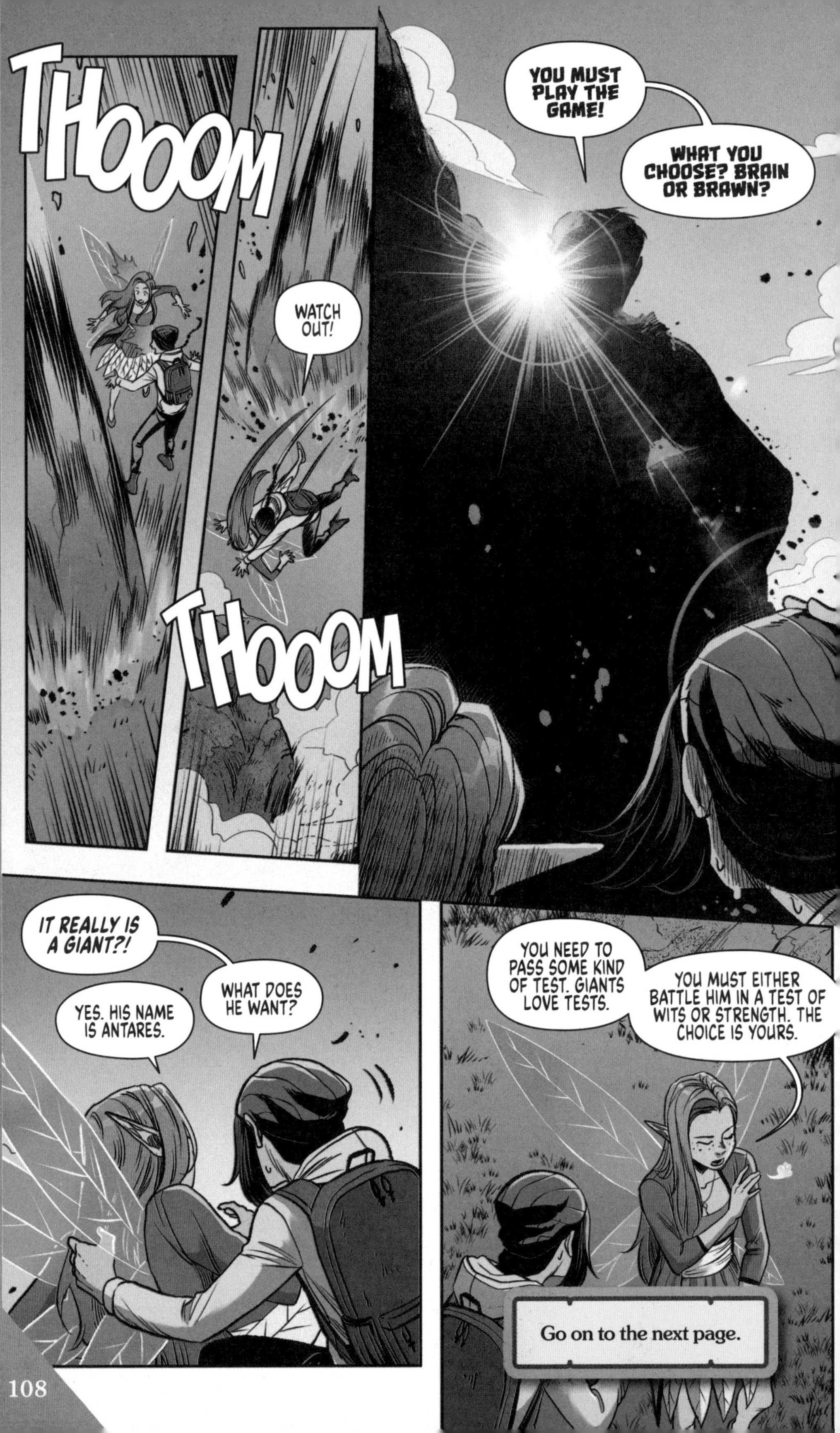
THOOOM
YOU MUST PLAY THE GAME!
WHAT YOU CHOOSE? BRAIN OR BRAWN?
WATCH OUT!
THOOOM
IT REALLY IS A GIANT?!
YES. HIS NAME IS ANTARES.
WHAT DOES HE WANT?
YOU NEED TO PASS SOME KIND OF TEST. GIANTS LOVE TESTS.
YOU MUST EITHER BATTLE HIM IN A TEST OF WITS OR STRENGTH. THE CHOICE IS YOURS.

Go on to the next page.

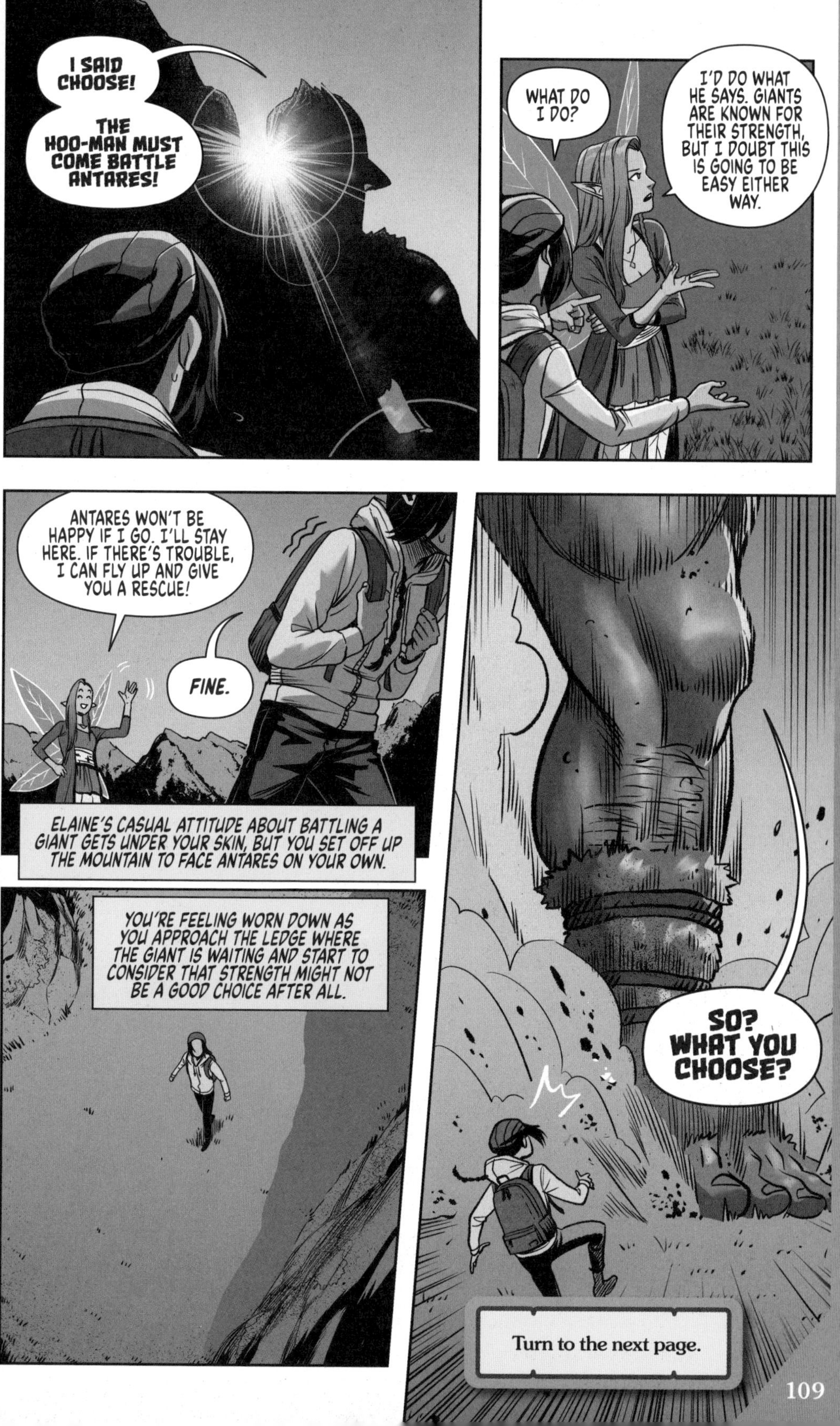
I SAID CHOOSE!
THE HOO-MAN MUST COME BATTLE ANTARES!
WHAT DO I DO?
I'D DO WHAT HE SAYS. GIANTS ARE KNOWN FOR THEIR STRENGTH, BUT I DOUBT THIS IS GOING TO BE EASY EITHER WAY.
ANTARES WON'T BE HAPPY IF I GO. I'LL STAY HERE. IF THERE'S TROUBLE, I CAN FLY UP AND GIVE YOU A RESCUE!
FINE.
ELAINE'S CASUAL ATTITUDE ABOUT BATTLING A GIANT GETS UNDER YOUR SKIN, BUT YOU SET OFF UP THE MOUNTAIN TO FACE ANTARES ON YOUR OWN.
YOU'RE FEELING WORN DOWN AS YOU APPROACH THE LEDGE WHERE THE GIANT IS WAITING AND START TO CONSIDER THAT STRENGTH MIGHT NOT BE A GOOD CHOICE AFTER ALL.
SO? WHAT YOU CHOOSE?

Turn to the next page.

BRAIN OR BRAWN? MAKE A CHOICE.

YOU LOOK UP AT THE GIGANTIC CREATURE BEFORE YOU, ALMOST UNABLE TO COMPREHEND THE QUESTION. THE SURPRISE OF HIS MASSIVE SIZE MOMENTARILY OVERWHELMS YOU.

ANTARES'S VOICE IS SO LOUD AND BOOMING YOU CAN FEEL IT IN YOUR BONES.

YOU SHAKE OFF THE SHOCK AND CONSIDER YOUR CHOICES...

If you decide to accept the giant's challenge to a test of brains, go on to the next page.

If you choose to challenge the giant in a test of strength, turn to page 115.

RIDDLE!

THERE IS A GREEN SINGLE-STORY HOUSE. EVERYTHING IN IT IS GREEN.

DOORS ARE GREEN, WINDOWS ARE GREEN, WALLS ARE GREEN...

I CHOOSE BRAIN.

BRAINS? WHY? YOU THINK I'M DUMB?

NO. I JUST THINK BRAINS IS MY ONLY CHANCE. I'M NOT A GOOD BRAWN CANDIDATE.

WHAT COLOR ARE THE STAIRS?

If you say green, turn to the next page.

If you try to think of another answer, turn to page 113.

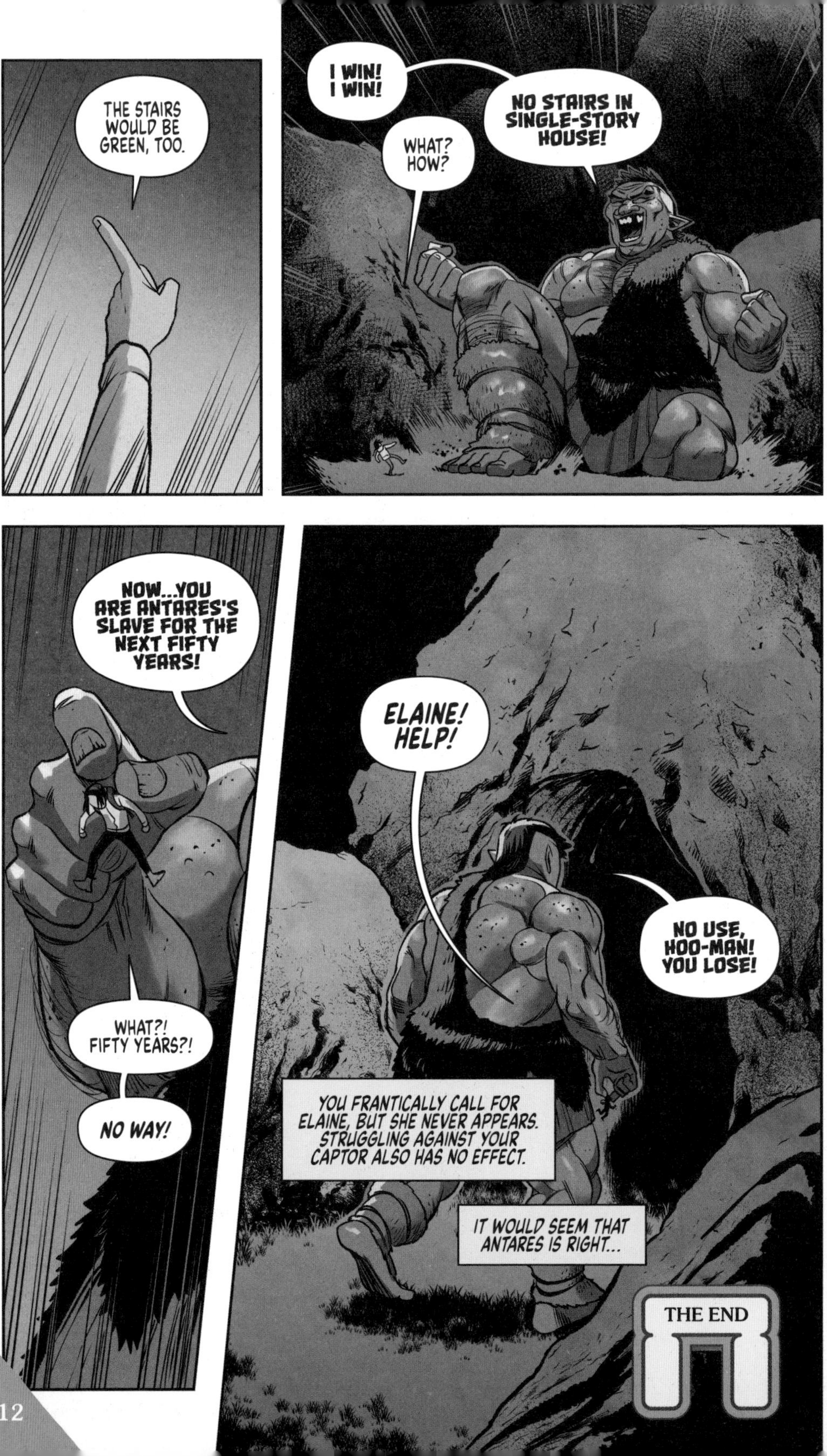
THE STAIRS WOULD BE GREEN, TOO.
I WIN! I WIN!
NO STAIRS IN SINGLE-STORY HOUSE!
WHAT? HOW?
NOW...YOU ARE ANTARES'S SLAVE FOR THE NEXT FIFTY YEARS!
WHAT?! FIFTY YEARS?!
NO WAY!
ELAINE! HELP!
NO USE, HOO-MAN! YOU LOSE!
YOU FRANTICALLY CALL FOR ELAINE, BUT SHE NEVER APPEARS. STRUGGLING AGAINST YOUR CAPTOR ALSO HAS NO EFFECT.
IT WOULD SEEM THAT ANTARES IS RIGHT...
THE END

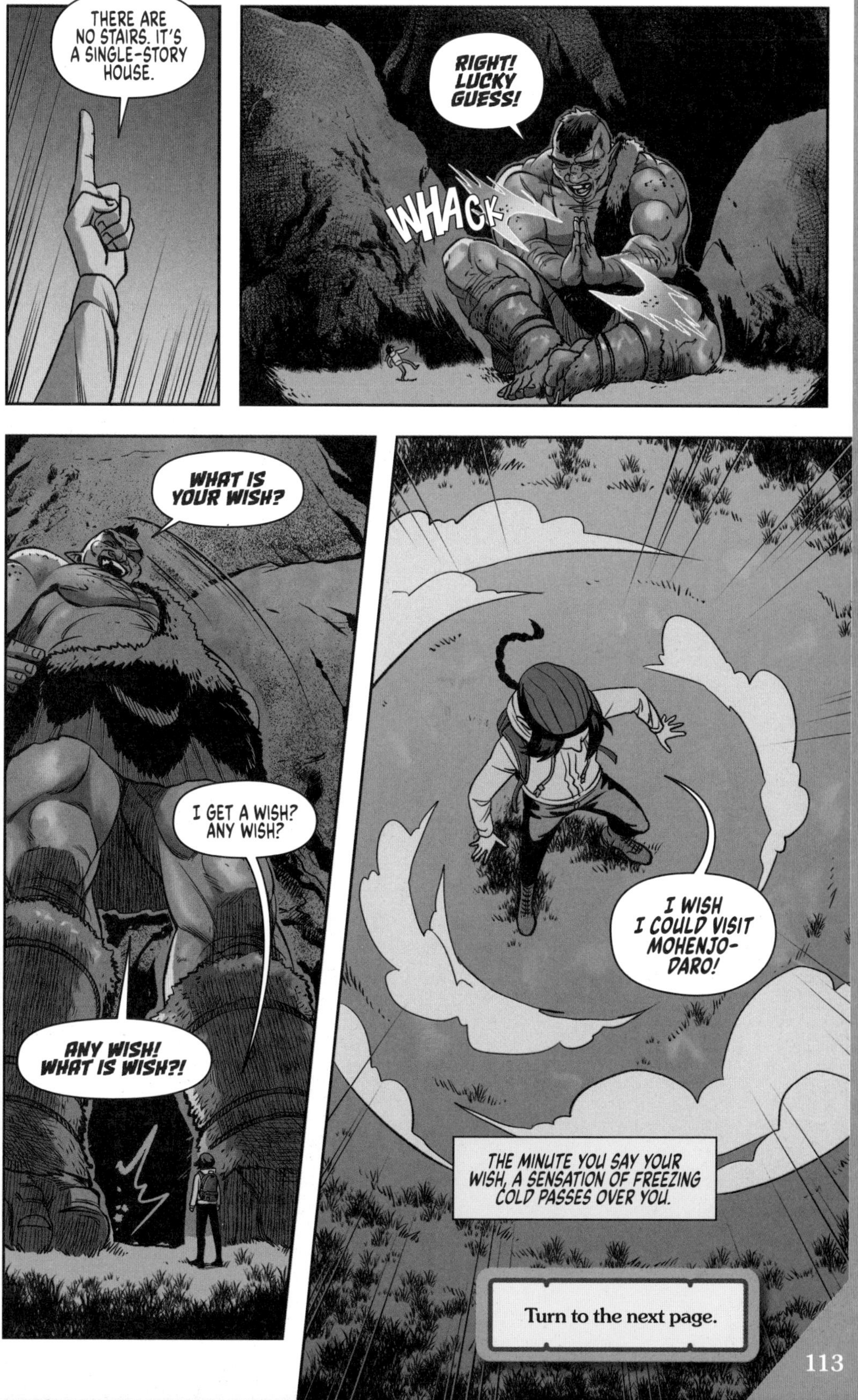
THERE ARE NO STAIRS. IT'S A SINGLE-STORY HOUSE.
RIGHT! LUCKY GUESS!
WHACK
WHAT IS YOUR WISH?
I GET A WISH? ANY WISH?
ANY WISH! WHAT IS WISH?!
I WISH I COULD VISIT MOHENJO-DARO!
THE MINUTE YOU SAY YOUR WISH, A SENSATION OF FREEZING COLD PASSES OVER YOU.

Turn to the next page.

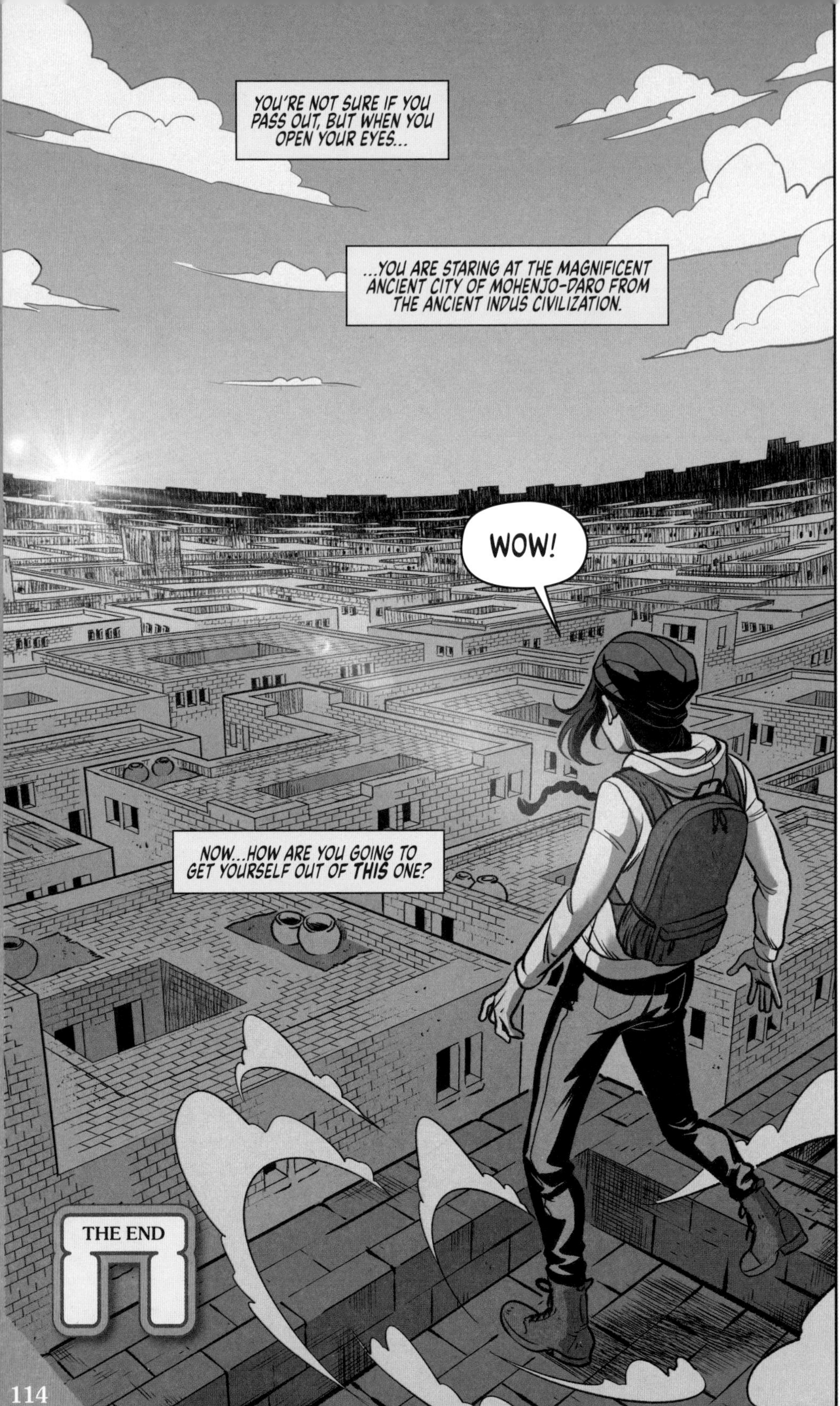
YOU'RE NOT SURE IF YOU PASS OUT, BUT WHEN YOU OPEN YOUR EYES...
...YOU ARE STARING AT THE MAGNIFICENT ANCIENT CITY OF MOHENJO-DARO FROM THE ANCIENT INDUS CIVILIZATION.
WOW!
NOW...HOW ARE YOU GOING TO GET YOURSELF OUT OF THIS ONE?
THE END

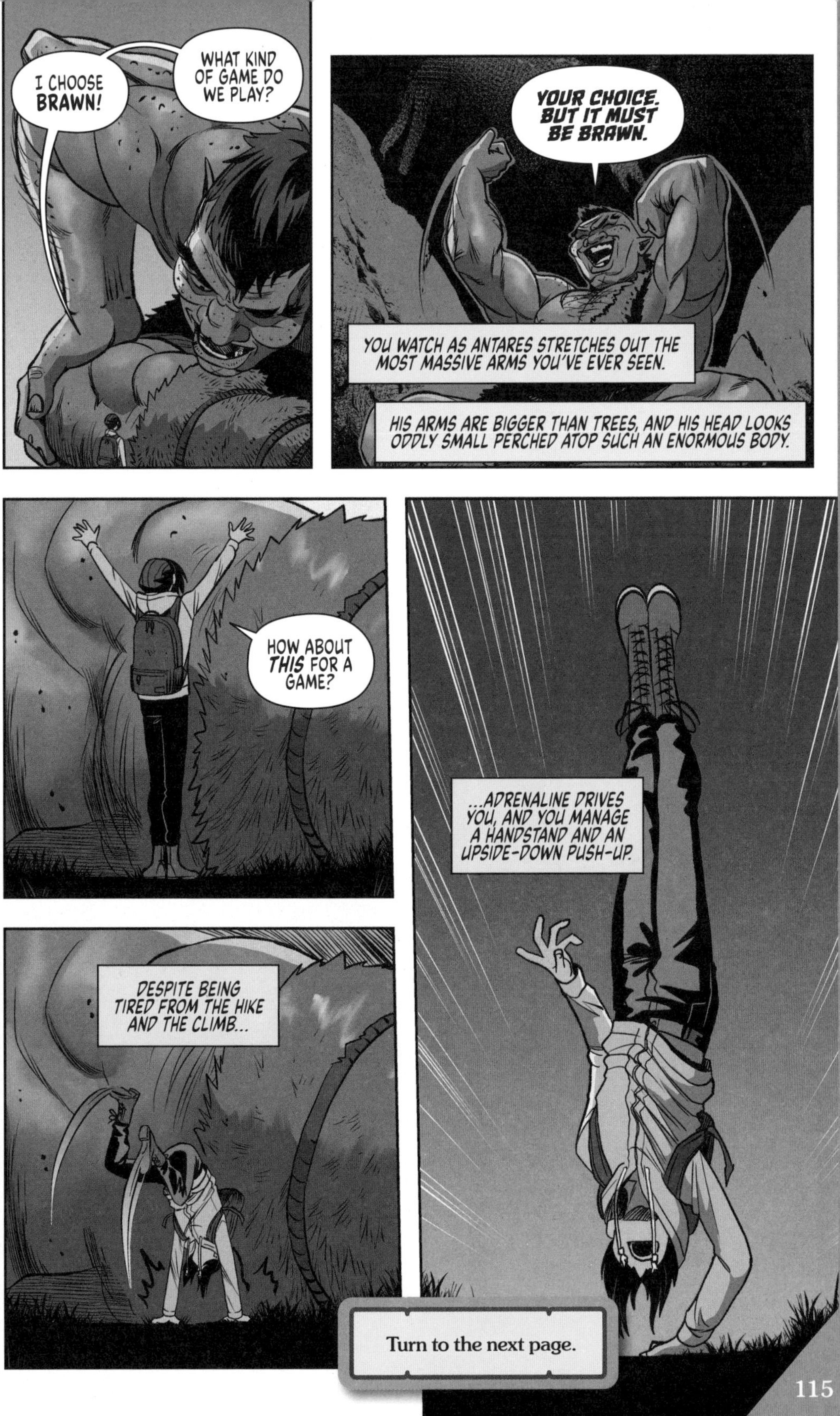
WHAT KIND OF GAME DO WE PLAY?
I CHOOSE BRAWN!
YOUR CHOICE. BUT IT MUST BE BRAWN.
YOU WATCH AS ANTARES STRETCHES OUT THE MOST MASSIVE ARMS YOU'VE EVER SEEN.
HIS ARMS ARE BIGGER THAN TREES, AND HIS HEAD LOOKS ODDLY SMALL PERCHED ATOP SUCH AN ENORMOUS BODY.
HOW ABOUT THIS FOR A GAME?
DESPITE BEING TIRED FROM THE HIKE AND THE CLIMB...
...ADRENALINE DRIVES YOU, AND YOU MANAGE A HANDSTAND AND AN UPSIDE-DOWN PUSH-UP.

Turn to the next page.

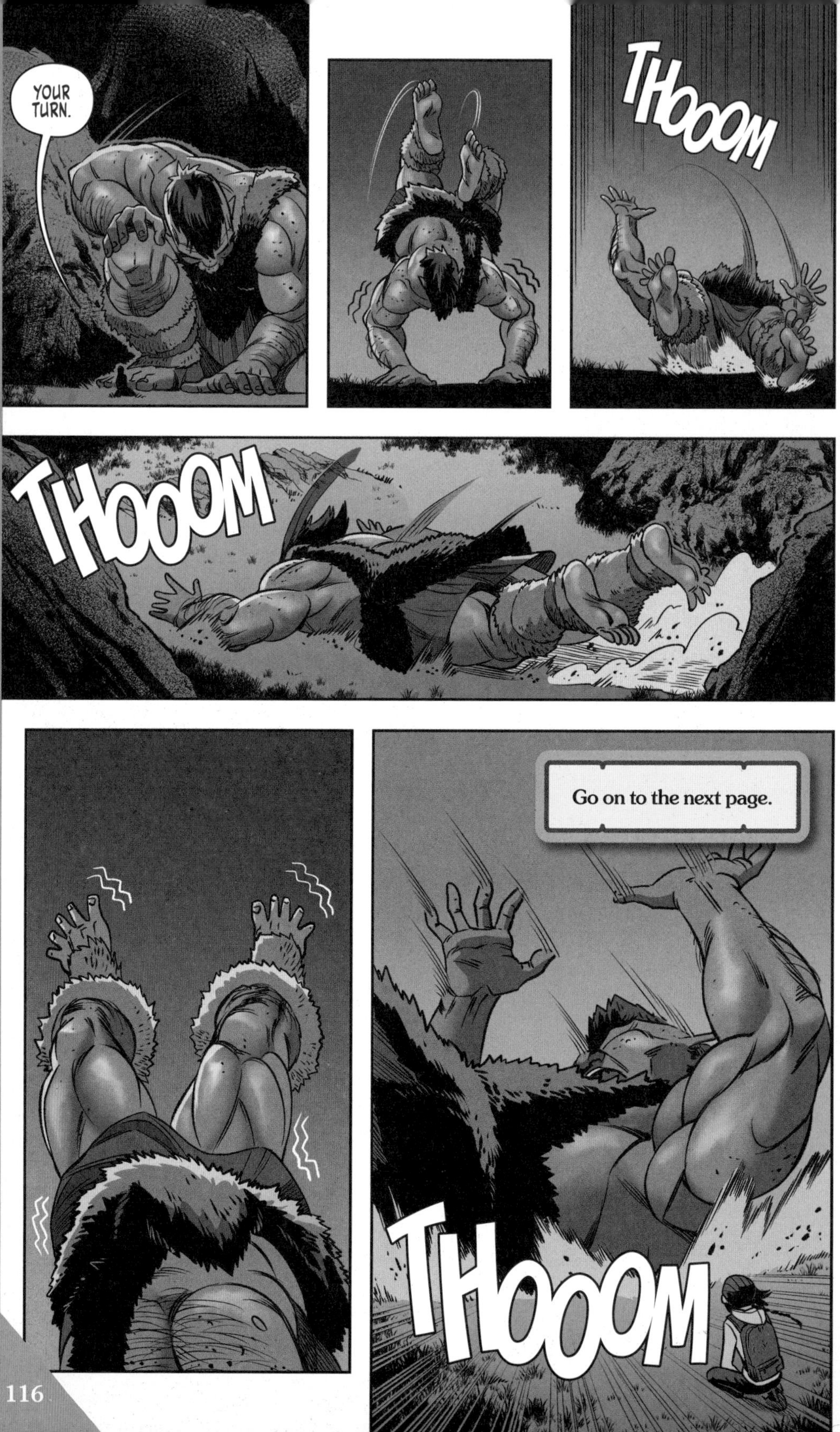
YOUR TURN.
THOOOM
THOOOM
Go on to the next page.
THOOOM

NOT SURE THAT IS ALL BRAWN, BUT YOU WON FAIR AND SQAURE.

I WILL NOT SMASH YOU.

SO WHY DID THE FAE SEND YOU?

THEIR QUEEN SAW A FORETELLING OF DOOM AT THE SOLSTICE LAST NIGHT. BUT HER VISION WAS CUT SHORT.

THE HENGE ENERGY IS *STUCK.* SHE THOUGHT THE ORIGINAL BUILDERS MIGHT KNOW HOW TO FIX IT. SHE NEEDS TO KNOW WHAT HAPPENS.

I DON'T KNOW ABOUT THE HOO-MAN STONEHENGE... I'M TOO YOUNG. BUT I KNOW WHERE THE REAL GIANTS' HENGE IS.

WE COULD TAKE A LOOK AT THAT AND SEE IF THAT HELPS YOU. OR...

OR WHAT?

I ALSO KNOW WHERE MERLIN LIVES. HE WAS SUPPOSED TO BE THE ONE WHO HELPED US TO DESIGN THE HENGES.

I WILL TAKE YOU TO EITHER ONE. WHICH WILL IT BE?

If you want to look for Merlin to find out the secrets of how the henges were built, turn to the next page.

If you decide to look at the giants' henge for clues on how to fix the human Stonehenge, turn to page 120.

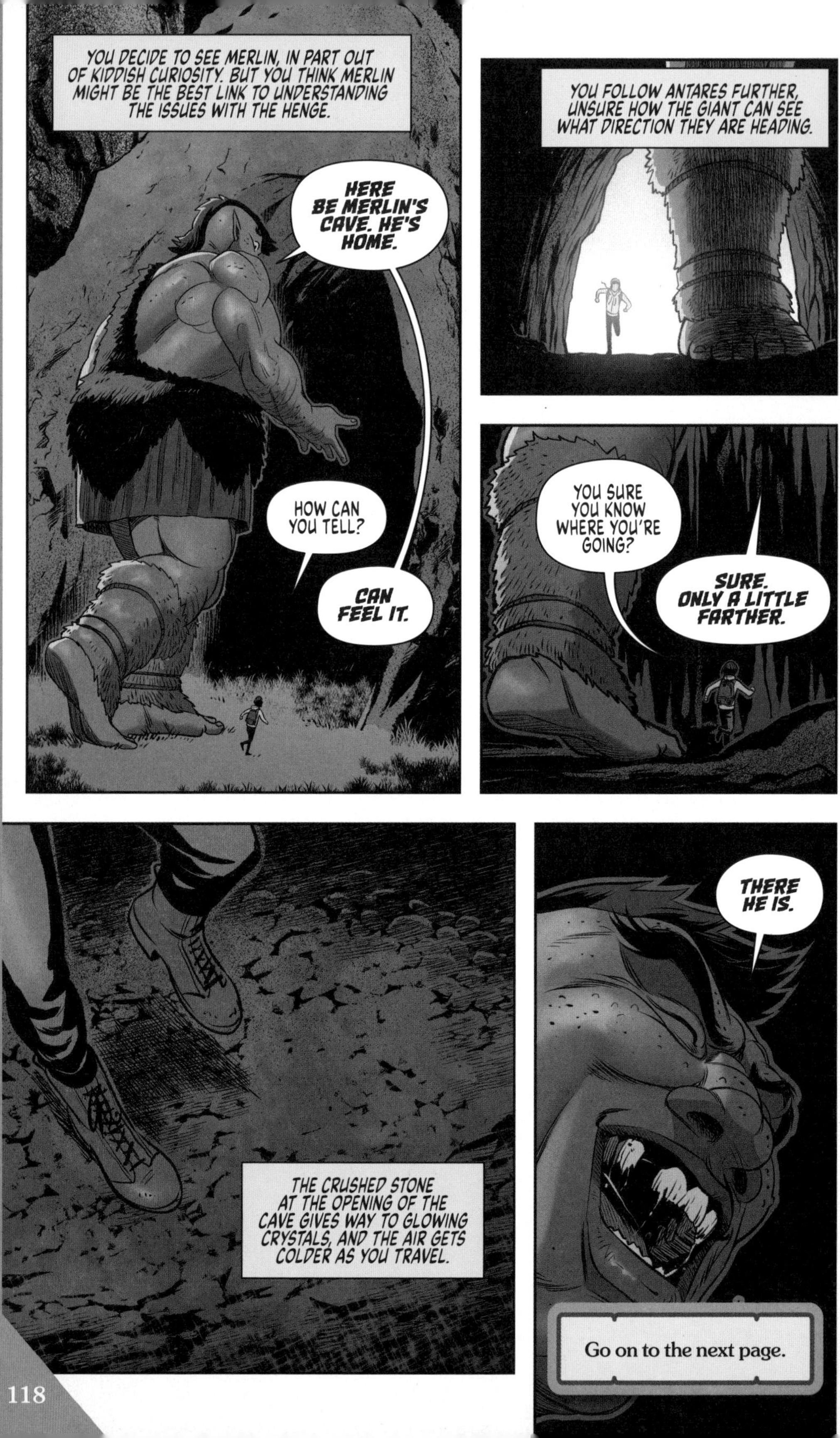

YOU DECIDE TO SEE MERLIN, IN PART OUT OF KIDDISH CURIOSITY. BUT YOU THINK MERLIN MIGHT BE THE BEST LINK TO UNDERSTANDING THE ISSUES WITH THE HENGE.
HERE BE MERLIN'S CAVE. HE'S HOME.
HOW CAN YOU TELL?
CAN FEEL IT.
YOU FOLLOW ANTARES FURTHER, UNSURE HOW THE GIANT CAN SEE WHAT DIRECTION THEY ARE HEADING.
YOU SURE YOU KNOW WHERE YOU'RE GOING?
SURE. ONLY A LITTLE FARTHER.
THE CRUSHED STONE AT THE OPENING OF THE CAVE GIVES WAY TO GLOWING CRYSTALS, AND THE AIR GETS COLDER AS YOU TRAVEL.
THERE HE IS.

Go on to the next page.

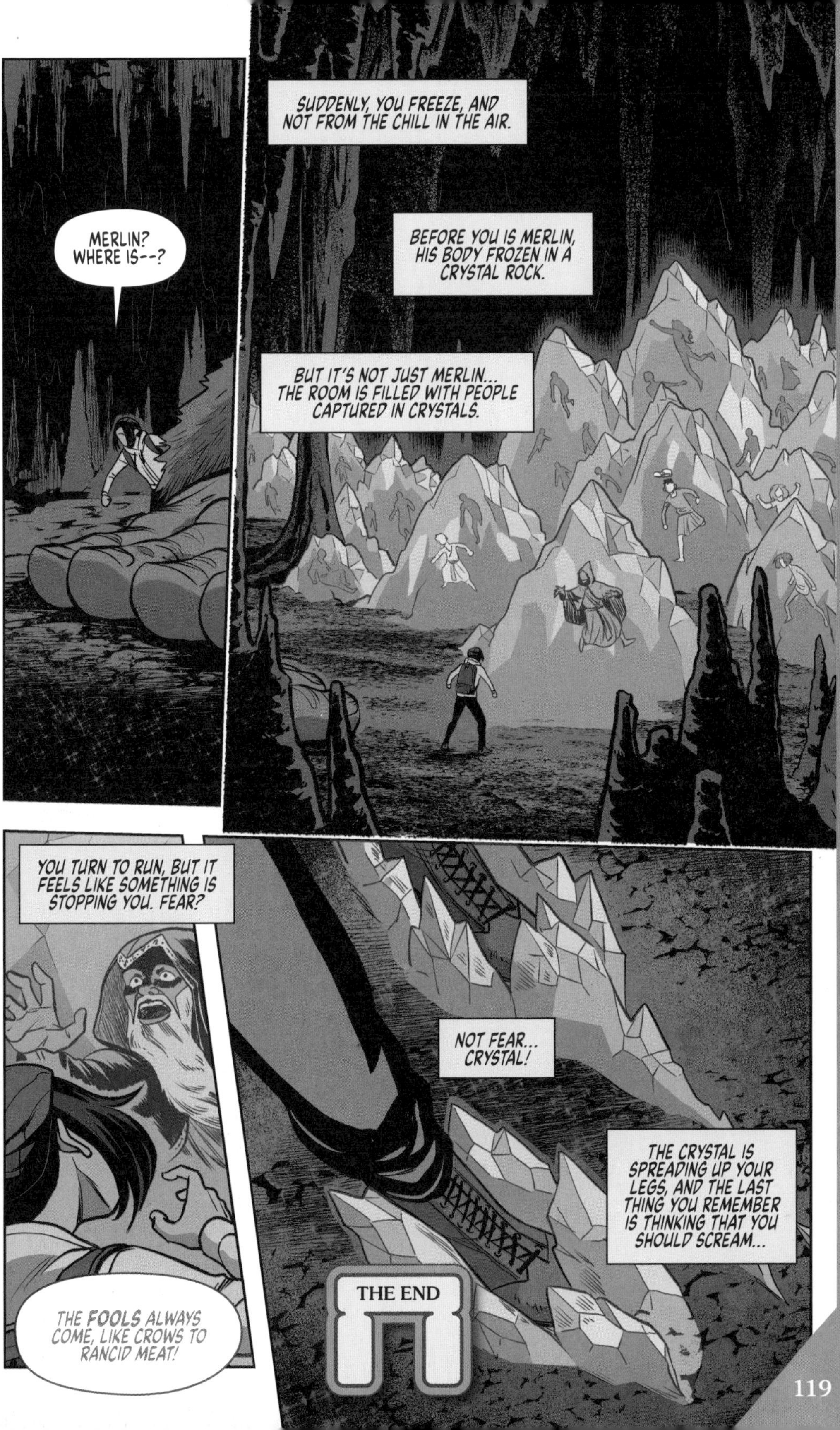
MERLIN? WHERE IS--?
SUDDENLY, YOU FREEZE, AND NOT FROM THE CHILL IN THE AIR.
BEFORE YOU IS MERLIN, HIS BODY FROZEN IN A CRYSTAL ROCK.
BUT IT'S NOT JUST MERLIN... THE ROOM IS FILLED WITH PEOPLE CAPTURED IN CRYSTALS.
YOU TURN TO RUN, BUT IT FEELS LIKE SOMETHING IS STOPPING YOU. FEAR?
THE FOOLS ALWAYS COME, LIKE CROWS TO RANCID MEAT!
NOT FEAR... CRYSTAL!
THE CRYSTAL IS SPREADING UP YOUR LEGS, AND THE LAST THING YOU REMEMBER IS THINKING THAT YOU SHOULD SCREAM...
THE END

YOU DECIDE TO TRY THE GIANTS' HENGE, AND ANTARES OFFERS TO GIVE YOU A RIDE.

YOU HOLD TIGHT ONTO SOME PART OF THE GIANT...MAYBE A SHIRT, OR A BIG FOLD OF SKIN.

YOU CLUTCH IT TIGHTLY, BUT THE RIDE IS SMOOTH DESPITE ANTARES'S LUMBERING BUILD.

IT'S HOURS BEFORE THE GIANTS' HENGE, GYYTNHENGE, COMES WITHIN VIEW.

THERE IT IS.

Go on to the next page.

120

THE HENGE IS AWESOME AND ENORMOUS. THERE ARE THREE RINGS OF STONE, THE SMALLEST OF THE STONES AT LEAST THIRTY FEET TALL.

IT'S HARD TO SEE INTO THE CENTER, BUT YOU THINK YOU SPOT A FIRE BURNING.

WITHOUT WARNING, YOU FEEL ANTARES'S MASSIVE HAND GRAB HOLD OF YOU...

...AND DROP YOU TO THE DEW-COVERED GRASS.

YOU WATCH CURIOUSLY AS ANTARES BOWS HIS HEAD BEFORE THE MASSIVE STONE STRUCTURE.

I PRAY THE GUIDES AND MASTERS, AND CHILDREN OF ALL WORLDS, TO GUIDE ME FORWARD AND BRING WISDOM, HEALING, AND BALANCE.

I HUMBLY REQUEST ENTRY INTO THE HENGE.

HELLO, ANTARES.

Turn to the next page.

121

FREYA?

YES, IT IS ME. I HAVEN'T SEEN YOU SINCE YOU AND YOUR BROTHER WERE CAUGHT STEALING HOGBOON MAGIC AT THE LAST CONCURRENCE. THAT MUST BE ALMOST FORTY YEARS...

WHAT BRINGS YOU HERE TODAY?

IF I KNEW YOU WERE WORKING MAGIC, I WOULD NOT HAVE BROUGHT A GUEST...

...MUCH LESS A HOO-MAN.

I'M NOT PERFORMING MAGIC, JUST ENERGY CLEANSING. BUT IT IS STRANGE TO SEE A HOO-MAN HERE.

TELL ME, HOO-MAN, WHAT BRINGS YOU HERE?

THE FAE QUEEN SENT THE YOUNGSTER. SHE HAS A DARK VISION OF THE FUTURE ON THE SOLSTICE.

BUT THE HOO-MAN HENGE WAS NOT SUPPLYING HER THE FULL PICTURE.

SHE SENT ME AS AN AMBASSADOR TO TRY TO FIND OUT WHY THE HENGE WON'T WORK.

THERE ARE SEVERAL PROBLEMS.

LET US GO SIT BY THE FIRE...

"THESE HENGES, BOTH GYYTNHENGE AND STONEHENGE, WERE BUILT ON ENERGY VORTEXES..."

Go on to the next page.

122

...PORTALS TO THE UNIVERSE WHERE ENERGY IMBALANCES COULD BE RIGHTED.

THIS WAS NEEDED BECAUSE OF THE NATURE OF *THOUGHT.*

YOU LISTEN INTENTLY TO FREYA, EVEN THOUGH YOU'RE NOT SURE YOU ENTIRELY UNDERSTAND WHAT SHE'S SAYING.

YOU SEE, THOUGHTS ARE *THINGS.* WHEN A PERSON HAS A THOUGHT, THE ENERGY OF THAT THOUGHT HANGS THERE IN SPACE. MOST THOUGHTS JUST HANG THERE...WAITING FOR LIKE THOUGHTS TO BIND WITH IT.

THE FIRE ILLUMINATES FREYA'S FACE AS SHE TALKS, AND YOU FEEL WARM IN HER PRESENCE, A WELCOME RELIEF.

ENOUGH BAD THOUGHTS BIND TOGETHER, AND EVENTUALLY THE BAD THING *ACTUALLY* HAPPENS ON THE PHYSICAL REALM.

THE HENGES WERE BUILT BY THE GUIDES TO REMEDY THIS AND CLEAR AWAY THE BAD ENERGY.

YOU SEE, MOST PEOPLE HAVE TROUBLE CONTROLLING NEGATIVE THOUGHTS, ESPECIALLY *HOO-MANS.*

YOU ARE BEGINNING TO UNDERSTAND. THOUGHTS ARE MORE POWERFUL THAN YOU EVER ANTICIPATED. YOU WISH YOU COULD TELL TWIG ABOUT IT.

THINGS WERE IMPROVING AT STONEHENGE UNTIL SOMEONE MOVED THE HEEL STONE.

SO TO RESTORE THE POWER OF STONEHENGE, THE HEEL STONE MUST BE RETURNED?

Turn to the next page.

THE WARMTH YOU FELT FROM THE FIRE SUDDENLY SPREADS, ALMOST AS IF THERE IS A BURNING SENSATION INSIDE YOUR VERY BODY.

THE HEAT SPREADS FROM YOUR CHEST AND THROUGH YOUR LIMBS UNTIL YOU FEEL A SUDDEN SLEEP PASSING OVER YOU...

...THEN EVERYTHING GOES BLACK.

Go on to the next page.

WHEN YOU WAKE, YOU ARE LYING ON YOUR BACK IN A GREEN FIELD. THERE'S A TINGLING SENSATION IN YOUR LIMBS, BUT NOTHING HURTS.

AS YOU SIT UP, YOU CAN SEE STONEHENGE IN THE DISTANCE AND THE CAR PARK JUST ACROSS THE WAY.

YOU'RE SITTING IN A SMALL DEPRESSION IN THE EARTH, AND IT SUDDENLY HITS YOU...

...YOU'VE LANDED IN THE VERY SPOT WHERE THE HEEL STONE ONCE STOOD.

WHERE'S TWIG? YOU'VE GOT WORK TO DO...

THE END

I WOULD LIKE TO TRY THE TROW, YOUR MAJESTY.

VERY WELL. THE TROW INHABIT THE HUMAN SIDE.

ELAINE CAN TAKE YOU, BUT BE CAUTIOUS OF THEIR TRICKS.

I WILL.

THIS WAY. THE TROW HAVE A SPECIFIC AREA NEAR STONEHENGE THEY RATHER LIKE.

WE'LL TRY THERE FIRST.

ELAINE PROCEEDS TO LEAD YOU THROUGH A COMPLEX SERIES OF NARROW TUNNELS THAT WIND UNDERNEATH THE EARTH.

Go on to the next page.

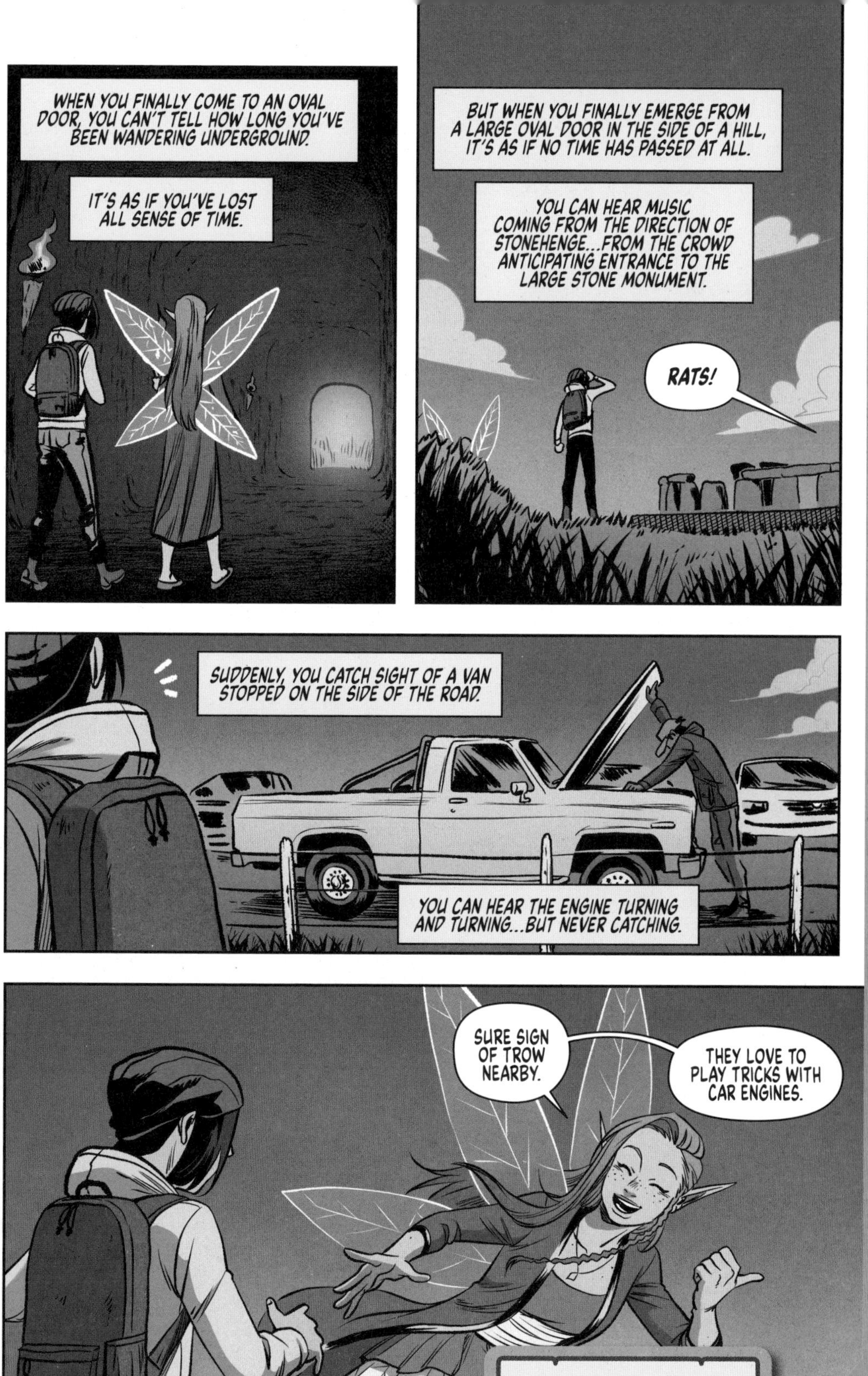

WHEN YOU FINALLY COME TO AN OVAL DOOR, YOU CAN'T TELL HOW LONG YOU'VE BEEN WANDERING UNDERGROUND.
IT'S AS IF YOU'VE LOST ALL SENSE OF TIME.
BUT WHEN YOU FINALLY EMERGE FROM A LARGE OVAL DOOR IN THE SIDE OF A HILL, IT'S AS IF NO TIME HAS PASSED AT ALL.
YOU CAN HEAR MUSIC COMING FROM THE DIRECTION OF STONEHENGE...FROM THE CROWD ANTICIPATING ENTRANCE TO THE LARGE STONE MONUMENT.
RATS!
SUDDENLY, YOU CATCH SIGHT OF A VAN STOPPED ON THE SIDE OF THE ROAD.
YOU CAN HEAR THE ENGINE TURNING AND TURNING...BUT NEVER CATCHING.
SURE SIGN OF TROW NEARBY.
THEY LOVE TO PLAY TRICKS WITH CAR ENGINES.

Turn to the next page.

YOU SPOT A QUICK FLASH OF DARK FUR AS THE GRASS AROUND YOU BEGINS TO RUSTLE.

Go on to the next page.

YOU SPEAK ENGLISH?

EVERY TROW DOES. IT'S OUR SECOND LANGUAGE. WE HAD TO USE IT TO HELP TRANSLATE THE HUMAN SPEECH WHEN WE BUILT THE HENGE.

BACK THEN, GIANTS DIDN'T KNOW A WORD OF IT.

THAT'S ACTUALLY WHY I CAME TO FIND YOU. I HAVE A QUESTION FROM THE FAE QUEEN ABOUT STONEHENGE.

WHAT? DON'T TELL ME SHE'S HAVING TROUBLE WITH HER VISIONS *AGAIN*?

AGAIN?

SHE HAS THE SAME TROUBLE *EVERY* YEAR. EVER SINCE THE STONES FELL OVER AND THE HUMANS PUT THEM BACK UP THE WRONG WAY.

PLANET HAS BEEN OUT OF BALANCE EVER SINCE. *PLAIN AND* SIMPLE.

WHAT CAN WE DO?

PUT THEM BACK THE RIGHT WAY, OF COURSE.

BUT FOR THAT, YOU'D NEED THE *PLANS.*

Turn to the next page.

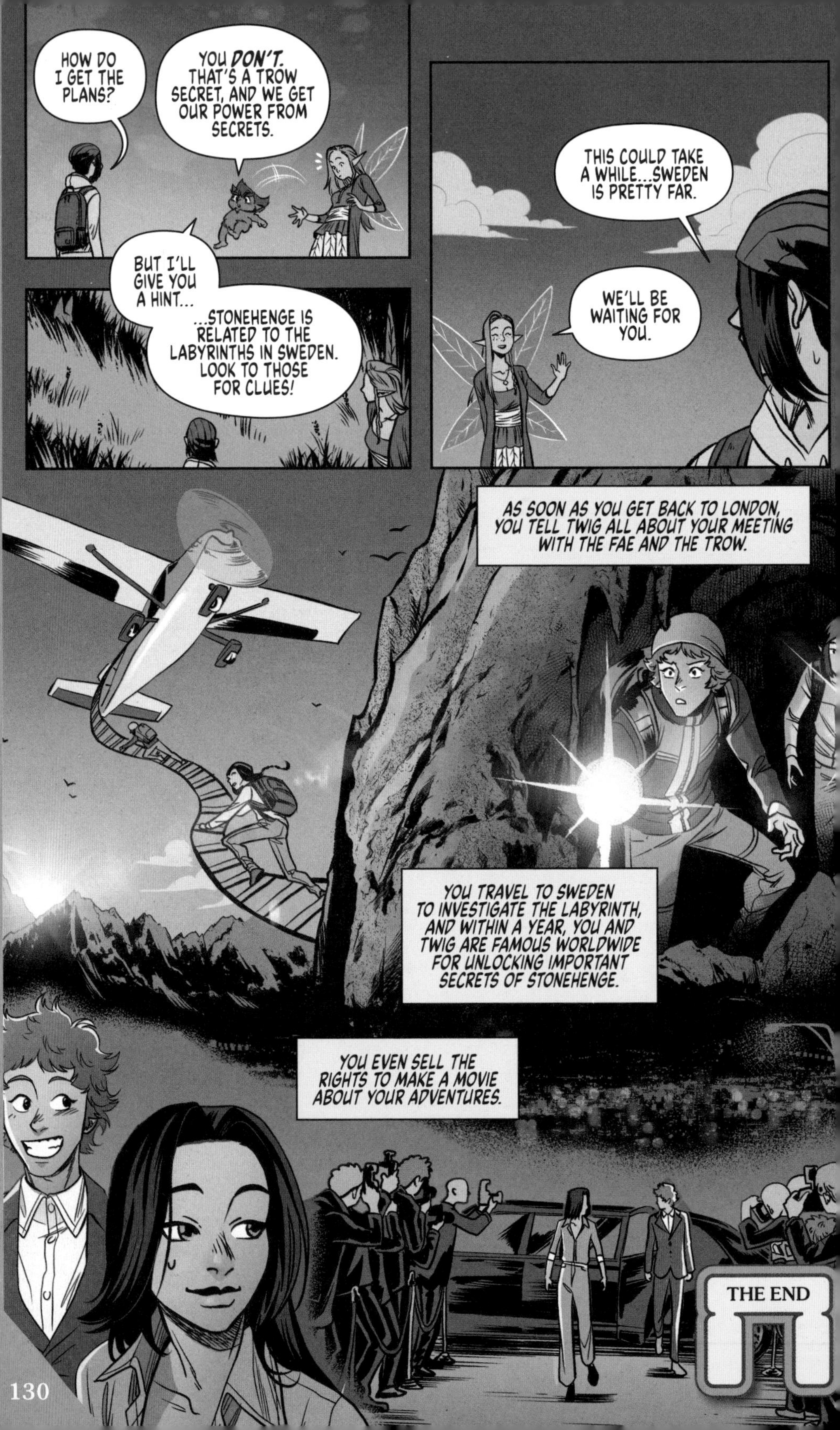
HOW DO I GET THE PLANS?
YOU ***DON'T***. THAT'S A TROW SECRET, AND WE GET OUR POWER FROM SECRETS.
BUT I'LL GIVE YOU A HINT...
...STONEHENGE IS RELATED TO THE LABYRINTHS IN SWEDEN. LOOK TO THOSE FOR CLUES!
THIS COULD TAKE A WHILE...SWEDEN IS PRETTY FAR.
WE'LL BE WAITING FOR YOU.
AS SOON AS YOU GET BACK TO LONDON, YOU TELL TWIG ALL ABOUT YOUR MEETING WITH THE FAE AND THE TROW.
YOU TRAVEL TO SWEDEN TO INVESTIGATE THE LABYRINTH, AND WITHIN A YEAR, YOU AND TWIG ARE FAMOUS WORLDWIDE FOR UNLOCKING IMPORTANT SECRETS OF STONEHENGE.
YOU EVEN SELL THE RIGHTS TO MAKE A MOVIE ABOUT YOUR ADVENTURES.
THE END

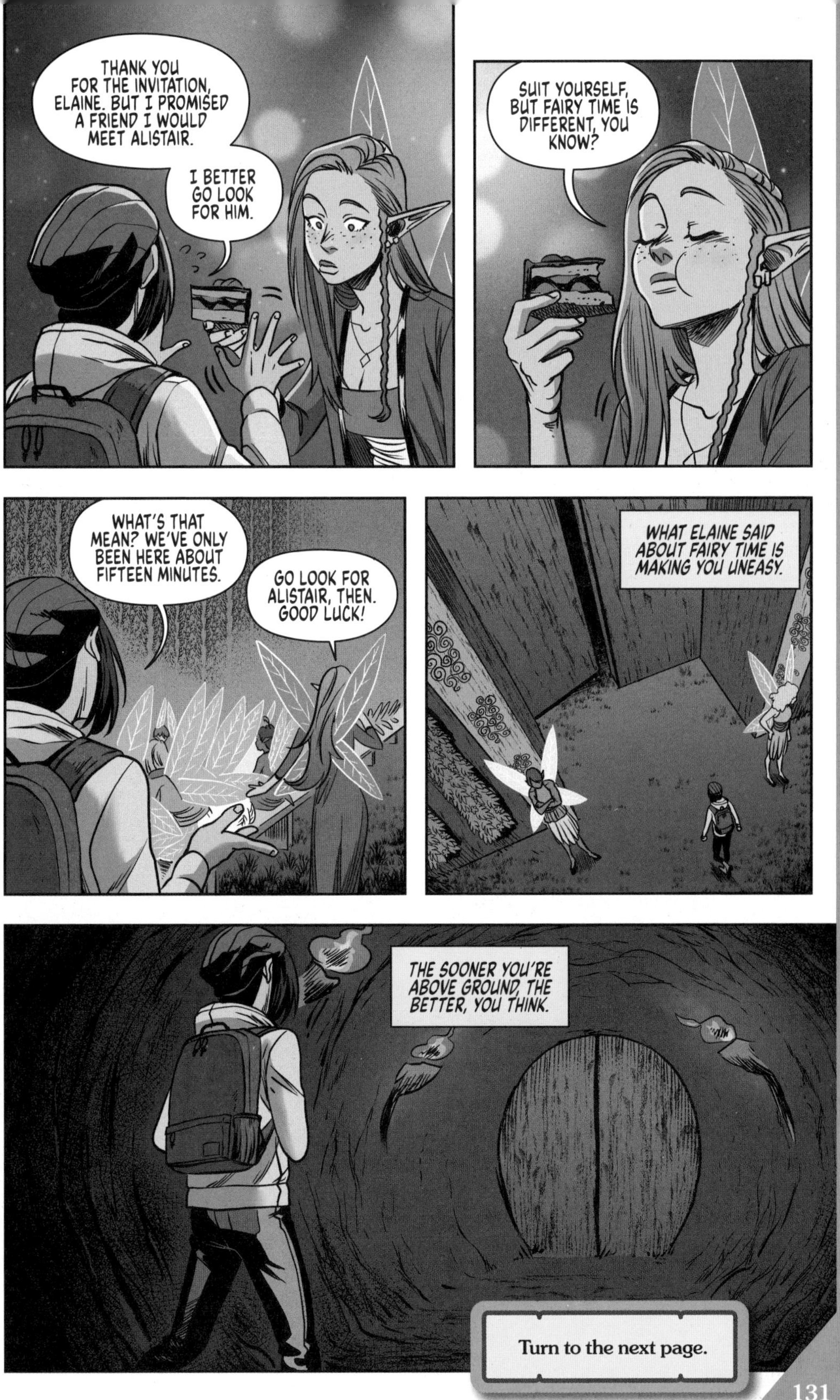
THANK YOU FOR THE INVITATION, ELAINE. BUT I PROMISED A FRIEND I WOULD MEET ALISTAIR.
I BETTER GO LOOK FOR HIM.
SUIT YOURSELF, BUT FAIRY TIME IS DIFFERENT, YOU KNOW?
WHAT'S THAT MEAN? WE'VE ONLY BEEN HERE ABOUT FIFTEEN MINUTES.
GO LOOK FOR ALISTAIR, THEN. GOOD LUCK!
WHAT ELAINE SAID ABOUT FAIRY TIME IS MAKING YOU UNEASY.
THE SOONER YOU'RE ABOVE GROUND, THE BETTER, YOU THINK.
Turn to the next page.

AS SOON AS YOU STEP OUTSIDE INTO THE GREEN FIELD, YOU SENSE THAT SOMETHING HAS CHANGED.

FOR STARTERS, THE TIME OF DAY IS ALL WRONG. IT NOW LOOKS LIKE IT'S THE AFTERNOON INSTEAD OF THE EARLY EVENING.

YOU TAKE A FEW STEPS FORWARD AND REALIZE THE CAR PARK IS GONE.

THE DOZENS OF PEOPLE WAITING TO GET INTO THE STONEHENGE MONUMENT ARE GONE.

THE ONLY LIVING THING SEEMS TO BE A HORSE-DRAWN CARRIAGE APPROACHING ON A NARROW DIRT ROAD.

EXCUSE ME!

WHAT HAPPENED TO EVERYONE?

EVERYONE? I HAVE NO IDEA WHAT YOU MEAN.

I AM IN AMESBURY, RIGHT? NEAR THE STONEHENGE MONUMENT?

RIGHT. AMESBURY, ENGLAND. 1844. ARE YOU LOST?

1844?

THE END

132

STEPHANIE PHILLIPS

Stephanie Phillips is an American writer known for comics and graphic novels such as *Harley Quinn*, *Batman: Legends of the Dark Knight*, *Sensational Wonder Woman*, and *The Butcher of Paris*. Her stories and comics have appeared with DC Comics, Marvel, AfterShock Comics, Dark Horse, Oni Press, Top Cow/Image Comics, Heavy Metal, and more. Stephanie also holds a PhD in English.

DANI BOLINHO

Dani Bolinho is the writer and draftsman for *Lobo Mau*, *Underground*, and *Desaventureiros*. Dani is also an award-winner in Japan at the Silent Manga Audition for the story *Tattoo* in 2018, and cofounder of the studio IndieVisivel Press.

PH GOMES

PH Gomes is a Brazilian colorist who has always been in love with comics, addicted to cinema, and is a father and lover of pop culture.

JOAMETTE GIL

Joamette Gil is an award-winning editor, cartoonist, and letterer extraordinaire. Her letters grace the pages of such Oni-Lion Forge titles as *Archival Quality*, *Girl Haven*, and, of course, *Mooncakes*! She's best known for her groundbreaking imprint P&M Press, home to *POWER & MAGIC: The Queer Witch Comics Anthology* and *HEARTWOOD: Non-binary Tales of Sylvan Fantasy*.

CHOOSE YOUR OWN ADVENTURE®

FORECAST FROM STONEHENGE

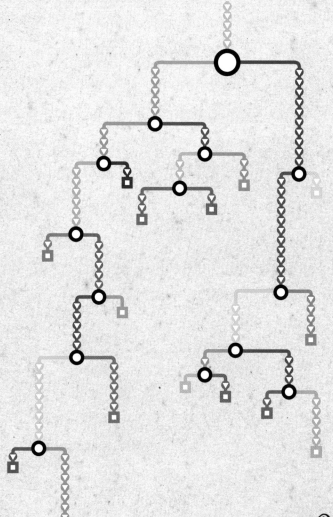

CHOOSECO

ONI PRESS

CHOOSE YOUR OWN ADVENTURE®

WITH GRAPHIC NOVELS

— R.A. MONTGOMERY PRESENTS —
CHOOSE YOUR OWN ADVENTURE®

JOURNEY UNDER THE SEA

Solve the mysteries of the ocean in the newest Choose Your Own Adventure® graphic novel! As a deep sea diver, you'll explore the ocean depths along with your crew on the scientific vessel the *Seeker*.

AVAILABLE NOW!

CHOOSE YOUR OWN ADVENTURE® 2

JOURNEY UNDER THE SEA

CHOOSE FROM 42 ENDINGS!

BY R. A. MONTGOMERY

Celebrating the 45th anniversary of the best-selling novel by R. A. Montgomery.

CHOOSECO